# PASSION PATROL SERIES

# SANTA

## BY

## EMMA CALIN

# SANTA

By Emma Calin

First published 2019

By Gallo-Romano Media

Copyright © 2019 Emma Calin

To the men and women of the Metropolitan Police at Christmas.

# TABLE OF CONTENTS

# SANTA

BY EMMA CALIN

# CHAPTER 1

Christmas? Who needed Christmas, for Christ's sake? Wasn't life difficult enough already?

Police Constable 866L, Paula Middleton, cruised the early evening streets of Brixton, South London, noting the houses with fairy lights and flashing neon reindeer in the front windows. The big bizz machine of buy, buy, buy had been at full power since Halloween. This year she just hadn't been able to capture the mood.

She swung the Ford Focus into the shadowy yard of Meadowchef Foods, a big wholesale supplier to cafés and restaurants. Trucks queued to load and unload at the line of warehouse doors. Mixed with the diesel smoke, flecks of icy sleet showed up in the headlamps. That's all she needed. Her assignment was routine. The manager wanted to discuss a hike in thefts. She parked the car and tried to find her professional concerned-and-interested face. She knew from experience that often the staff were the principal suspects. The wages here were low, the staff shifting and often without immigration papers. They would watch a cop show up and just maybe think twice before they stole again. No one would thank her for turning over too many stones.

There was a shout, and dodging between the trucks was a running male figure, clasping something under his jacket. In her soul she sighed. She was forty-one years old, thirteen years of service, and still on the bottom rank. Did she still have the dynamism to chase this guy alone, out into the dark streets? She was a cop. She had to be something genuine.

She was breathing hard, but gaining. The guy was still clutching his prize inside his jacket, making it hard for him to run. He hadn't looked round and maybe didn't know she was behind in the shadows. As a community officer she knew many of the local citizens, criminal or otherwise. There was something familiar about the guy ahead of her. She was still gaining and had gotten close enough to see he was limping. In a few seconds she would have a hand on his collar.

"Leroy, Leroy Prentice. I'm getting too old for this."

The suspect took another few steps and then paused as she came to a halt at his side.

"Leroy, you're under arrest, OK. Your poor bloody mother's going to go ballistic."

He hung his head, breathing hard.

"I told her I'd bring in something to eat."

"So you went thieving?"

He nodded.

"I'm on a suspended jail sentence. Please. Please. If you nick me I'm locked up."

"Why ain't you got any money?"

"The rent, the..."

"The blow, the crack or what?"

Leroy stared at the floor. As far as she could remember he was nineteen. Paula knew the family well. His mom, Melissa, was on her own and had been since Leroy was a baby. She had a younger boy Benny, with learning issues.

"What have you got in your coat?"

"Nothing."

"Just show me."

He pulled out a pack of catering quality burgers, two frozen pizzas and a pack of processed chopped chicken meat.

"Was it worth getting sent back to jail for that load of crap?"

The lad stared at his old torn trainers.

"How's your mom and Benny?"

"OK."

"Just fuck off, Leroy. Just get home and say nothing. You didn't get caught. This never happened, OK. Stay out of Meadowchef's yard. Do you understand?"

"What?"

"Keep the food and just fuck off. Like now."

He didn't need any more encouragement. He'd just made it to the next junction when she heard running footsteps behind her. It was a small man in shabby suit with an overweight security guard.

"That was him. He's getting away," said the guard.

"I stopped a guy but it wasn't your man."

"Yeah, that was him. Boss, that was him."

Paula kept calm. She was in the shit, but it wouldn't be the first time.

"Look, he was a young black guy. This is Brixton; who else are you going to see?"

"No, I saw you all the way. I couldn't quite get off the loading bay fast enough to catch you up."

"That's 'cause you're a useless fat bastard," said the small guy.

She smiled at him. He was a pale middle-aged man with smoke-stained teeth and a wispy dandruff-speckled comb over. Just for the moment he could be George Clooney.

"Nice to meet you, sir. I'm Paula, your community officer."

"I'm Nigel, logistics manager. Shall we go back to my office?"

"Only if you'll get me a nice cup of tea, Nigel. An officer always needs places where she can get some friendly company."

Nigel smiled, but the guard was still excited.

"Boss, that was the guy. She let him go."

"The officer has told you he wasn't so that's an end to that. Get back on your patrol."

They walked in silence back to the depot. The security guy peeled off still mumbling.

"He was only trying to do his job, Nigel. It's an honest mistake to make in the dark."

"Paula, I'm the boss here. A lot of these idle bastards are useless, including that slob. This place would be nothing without me. If I can ever help you, or if you'd like a few sausages, or a nice bit of beef? We'll have turkeys in next week so just come to me."

His expression had become almost a leer as he surveyed her body. She could definitely resist both his meat and his sausages. Just for now she'd play along. They walked through the depot, dodging fork trucks and grubby workers carrying trays of blood-dripping meat and chickens. He opened a door to an untidy damp smelling windowless office and took a seat behind a grey metal desk. She took a seat to face him.

"So Nigel, you've got an issue with theft."

"Yeah. All that lot out there are thieves, a load of scuzzbuckets and scumbags. We search them all the time. We've got hidden cameras in the toilets to watch them poking bags of frozen prawns and hot dogs into their stinking underwear. They throw stuff over the walls, they hide stuff under the trucks. We caught some of them munching frozen doughnuts they'd hidden next to their skin to thaw out. They're morons, Paula. People like you and me, you know, from the educated executive class, we know what these people are."

She wanted to keep him on her side, but couldn't find any suitable words.

"Does your human relations department deal with these issues?"

Nigel let out a cracked metallic snort.

"What? Human relations for that lot? The guv'nor hires and fires. He relies on me to keep this shit-hole turning over."

"And who's the guv'nor?"

"Max Muswell."

"Why do I know that name?"

The manager sniggered.

"Loads of people know Mr Muswell, including a lot of your top bosses. He runs training stables for racehorses. He was on the TV when his horse beat the Queen's in the Derby last year."

"Why does he want this business?"

"Money, Paula, money. He picked it up for nothing. He's nationwide these days. He's undercut all the others and raced them to the bottom and deeper. He's brought in low-cost labor on zero-hour contracts, he's scrapped the pension scheme, he uses self-employed drivers. You know, guys who push to the limits and aren't too difficult, if you know what I mean."

She knew very well what he meant. This guy was incredible. He was so keen to big himself up to a woman that he'd expose the shady operation of Meadowchef Foods for an ounce of kudos. Maybe her looks and size 16 charms still had some traction.

"He sounds very single minded and progressive."

"He's a hard man to beat. You must have read about his divorce?"

"Juicy divorce stories aren't my idea of entertainment. It was bad enough going through my own."

"His wife was that actress Azzura Vermillion. Christ Almighty, she was a right old brass, took him for everything and left him with her kid, some brat she had by Romano Poxato the film director."

"Yeah, I sort of remember that. I really should get out more."

"Just imagine, your missus going over the side, getting herself pregnant and then handing you the babe."

For a moment she reflected on what must have been a personal tragedy. For sure she would be Googling the scandalous details later. The guy in front of her didn't seem bothered about the Leroy Prentice incident. She wanted to stay professional.

"You believe your theft problem is mainly staff then. Where do you recruit them?"

"Well, Paula, you and I are practical people. There's a couple of business gentlemen who specialize in providing flexible labor solutions to our type of company. Mr Muswell prides himself on providing employment for many who would not otherwise find any work."

"Like you have to accept the people they supply?"

Nigel gave a thin smile.

"I can see you understand," he said.

Indeed she understood. Traffickers presented illegal immigrants to companies and took a big wedge of the wages as an old-fashioned protection racket. The workers were effectively slaves and had no choice. With no papers they could hardly escape and run to the police. Shortage of housing and high rents meant that regular low-skilled workers couldn't live in London.

"I'm guessing you don't want police to interview any of your workers?"

"Nah, fucking hell not. Look, Paula, most of them don't speak English. We can deal with these creatures ourselves. Mr Muswell wants to keep out those thieving bastards from the Loughborough estate. At Christmas this place is rammed with stuff and every toe-rag in London has got this sort of place on his list. If the cops can lock up a few, it'll put the others off. Between you and me he's threatening to put some loose Doberman dogs in the yard."

"Nigel, I couldn't support that. Loose guard dogs are against the law. A kid could get torn to shreds."

"Yeah, well, I'm just saying, you know. Come on, Paula, we're on your side against this scum."

She replied with a weak nod of her head. This guy was in her lifetime top ten of repulsive men. He continued.

"Now what about that tea? I expect you've got cozy tea spots on your patrols, Paula? If you ever needed just to rest your feet I've got a little nest upstairs for when I'm here at night. Maybe you work nights yourself sometimes?"

She watched his leering eyes sweep up and down her body. His mouth raised on one side revealing his brown teeth. He stood up and brushed past her to go a table behind her. His stained clothes smelled of animal blood, vegetables, and diesel fuel.

"I believe you said you aren't married yourself?"

His phlegm-rattled voice licked her like a cold lizard's tongue. She felt vulnerable and dirty. He looked up from pouring the tea.

"Quite amazing that no one's snapped you up. Many men—real men I think, like a bit of flesh on a woman."

Fuck! She needed to slap this man down, but also needed to keep him sweet. Why the hell had she let Leroy go? She knew why but this was not the moment to reflect upon her wider life. She stayed quiet while he restarted his sales pitch.

"And, may I say, prices are shooting up. A nice turkey, a supreme quality pudding and maybe a nice sack of Brussel sprouts could be a big help at Christmas?"

Paula started to laugh.

"Some girls get offered diamonds, others gold. How could a girl resist a man with a sack of brussel sprouts?"

Nigel let out a metallic whinny.

"Not being rude mind, not saying anything personal, but a little helping hand, a small act of friendship between executive-level people is normal. It's a shame that thieving bastard got away 'cause at first I thought you'd caught him. I know you cops don't want all that paperwork. I'd have done the same myself if you know what I mean. You take them to court and the fucking do-gooders let them walk free."

Shit. Shit, shit, shit. She was too soft for this job. She knew it and the bosses knew it. She thought back to her first days on the beat with her tutor constable Bob Lakin. He was an old sweat from the politically incorrect engine room, a survivor, a thief taker and a bit of a bruiser. He'd given her a bit of advice she'd never forgotten but never really used until now. *"If you have to tell a lie, tell it with confidence and just keep telling it. Once you've lied that lie is your truth. Never ever go back. They'll hang you for your honesty and take an extra rung on their career ladder. Never ever go back."*

"The guy I stopped was just a passerby. You were a long way back in the dark, Nigel."

"Yeah, well we'll keep it confidential between ourselves. eh?"

"No. The man I stopped was nothing to do with Meadowchef Foods. That's it."

He came back to his seat at the desk, handing her a greasy-feeling mug. She glanced at a picture of a naked grossly obese woman holding a bag of hamburger buns. The slogan read "Nice Rolls."

"Nah, like I'm just saying, Paula. A nod's as good as wink if you know what I mean? When I was a kid the copper would just slap you one in the mouth. Them days was better."

She considered the possibility of a copper slapping him straight in the mouth with immediate effect. She had to negotiate her way out of this situation with honor.

"Nice tea, thank you."

"A gorgeous woman is always welcome to the best catering blend we've got."

"I feel honoured, Nigel. I'll notify mobile patrols of your issues here and step up our attention to your yard. It seemed to me anyone can just walk in off the street."

"Yeah, we've got trucks in and out all day and all night. We've got CCTV and barbed wire protecting all the walls. We could do with high voltage live wires but it's not allowed is it?"

"No."

Without warning the office door barged open.

"There's a fucking police car in my parking bay," said a strong male voice in a broad East-End cockney accent.

She turned to see a tall man in his mid-to-late forties. His hair was cropped quite short, his cheek was scarred, and his nose a little deflected. His skin had a rugged outdoor look. Her eyes flicked to his Rolex watch, a chunky ruby ring on his finger, and the beautiful fit of his blue Chester Barrie Savile Row suit.

She stood up to offer her hand to shake. He didn't respond but looked her up and down.

"Your car then, is it?"

"Yeah."

"Well, I need it shifted."

"I think you need to get a few manners."

"Fucking what? This is my depot, my business, and my parking bay. I've got a new Rolls Royce out there with fucking morons swerving trucks round it. If one of those braindead monkeys dents my motor, your boss is going to get the bill."

His eyes were deep-set and at the dark end of hazel.

"My bosses are villains. They don't pay bills."

"Yeah, tell me about it, officer. You lot are the biggest gang of crooks in London."

She offered her hand once more. He took it and gripped it with an edge of anger.

"Nice to meet you, Mr Muswell."

"Yeah, yeah, yeah. Now move that heap of shit out of my bay."

"I take it you don't want me to introduce myself?" she said.

"You have. You're a copper and you're on my turf, that's it."

"In the absence of any courtesy I'll leave my card. I'm Paula Middleton, your community officer."

"Look sweetheart, I want you out of my bay. If you want to see me, make an appointment. The only thing you lot are good at is drinking tea. I'll apologize for swearing in the presence of a lady. Christ knows what good a woman can do on these streets. I pay a huge wedge of tax and I get nothing back."

"Well, maybe I'll use some taxpayer's money to pull over a couple of your trucks and check their driver's hours records, tires, and licenses."

"Don't threaten me. Those punch bags run their own trucks. Do what you like with them, there's plenty more where they come from."

Paula sighed inwardly. In less than one hour she'd met not only the most repulsive man of a lifetime, but also the most obnoxious.

"If you have any problems you can always call me. I'll get you an appointment or I can come round, if there's a parking space. The hardworking taxpayer buys those cars."

"Like you care, sweetheart. You lot get a good pension while business people like me have to graft and pay right up to the grave."

"I'm always pleased to meet a true conscientious taxpayer, Mr Muswell."

"Let's go. I can't waste any more time."

She walked with him through the depot. The staff looked dishevelled, pale, and thin.

"I believe your personnel are provided by an agency of some kind?"

"What's that to you? You just stick to plodding the beat."

"You just stick to answering my question. Your manager asked me in to discuss theft, including theft by your own staff. How do you source your workers?"

"Through an agency, a legit business that's none of your affair."

Large high flood lamps illuminated the yard. The wind was cold and flecked with sleet. She couldn't miss the silver and maroon Rolls-Royce Wraith coupe behind her humble Ford Focus. This guy was a bully, but she'd already sensed a weak point.

"If ever you want to talk about your labor situation, maybe I can help."

He paused and looked into her eyes. There was an anger inside him which could beat another man without a fight. She'd charged into bars and pubs too often in her life to confront such men. While his alpha dominance could deflate a man, a woman provided a moving target. This was a guy whose anger was defensive and maybe self-destructive. His aggression was attractive to a woman and he knew it, wanted her to see more, was almost inciting her to push further. It was crazy, but there was just a little surge inside her.

"Let me stick to being a billionaire business man. You get back to the station and write blah, blah, blah on five hundred bits of paper."

"Now you're talking my language. It's always great to meet someone who understands your problems, isn't it?"

He looked her up and down, a smile on his lips.

"I think it said Paula on your card."

"It did. I think your name is Max. If you ever want to chat about issues with the guys who supply your workforce you just give me a call, Max. Sometimes it's good to talk to someone who wants to listen while you've still got the chance. You never know what's round the corner."

"You coppers are always trying to worm your way into people's business."

She'd had a gutful of this jerk.

"Mister, let's call a spade a spade. Those people in there are dirty and hungry. You're a tough guy all right. I can fucking see that and you ain't any sort of pushover. I'll be honest. I don't think you want that situation, but thugs bigger than you ain't giving you a choice. You're Mister ruthless business man, blah, blah, blah as you put it. You've got serious organized bastards on your back. When you want to talk, call me. Now get that fucking great steel penis-substitute out of my way and I'll leave you to think."

"You've got some nerve."

"I'm glad you see that."

"It's a crying shame you're a cop."

"That's what all the villains say."

He laughed, showing perfect dental presentation. He was an attractive man except for his bullying patronizing personality.

"Just sod off and leave me to run my business."

She turned and went to her vehicle.

"Have a nice day," she added.


Before she went off duty, she ran a criminal records check on Mr Max Muswell. Sure enough he popped up as known to police for a minor bar-room fight assault when he was twenty-two. Somehow since then he'd stayed out of trouble or had the cash to pay good lawyers. He didn't look like a man afraid of a fight.

# CHAPTER 2

She'd never been so glad to get home. She had to soak out the leering dirty atmosphere of Nigel the manager and Meadowchef Foods. The boss had been a different matter all together. Toward Max Muswell she felt nothing but anger, bordering on rage. Her feelings were made worse by his attractiveness. How could she be drawn to a vile piece of shit like him? All the same she could see how a woman would like his tough-guy looks and his tall, bull-bodied confidence. Some woman like an actress with no brains or morals.

While she heated water for a bath she poured a large glass of Rockstone Red Californian wine. She powered up her laptop and googled Max Muswell. There was no shortage of information. She skipped to the section on his infamous divorce. Apparently he'd fallen for Azzura Vermillion, a porn star with a real name of Wendy Wiggins from Dagenham, East London. He'd funded all manner of enhancements and reshaping and had gotten her into the mainstream movie business. They got married and all seemed well. She was making a film with the womanizing Romano Poxato on location in Istanbul. Seemingly, she offered her charms to him for a one-night gig and returned pregnant to her loving Max when the filming was completed. He commented on her slight increase in size but believed her explanation that the movie had required her to play the part of a belly dancer. As a true professional she'd eaten lamb kebabs with a box of Turkish Delight chocolate as dessert every day. Seemingly there was laughter in the divorce court. Max Muswell told the press he felt humiliated by his gullibility, but that he'd loved her so much he wanted to believe her.

Azzura Vermillion attempted to disguise her pregnancy with corsets but finally fled to Romano Poxato's villa in the Bahamas, where he had installed a French teenage actress with a view to giving her screen tests. He turned his back on Azzura and she wound up in a hospital in Miami having given birth to a premature infant alone in a motel room. She abandoned the babe at the hospital and instructed lawyers to sue Max Muswell for divorce on the grounds of cruelty. Sidelined by Romano Poxato, she never objected to Max becoming the sole parent.

She clicked through his early life. Zero academically. He'd made some money as a fighter in unlicensed boxing in the East End of London. He'd made and lost a million as a professional gambler by the time he was twenty-five. He'd bought some racehorse stables during the good times and built a multi-million-dollar training and stud business. After his divorce he'd gone back to backstreet fighting, in his own words, to deal with his anger issues. He'd wound up injured and while recovering bought the bankrupt Meadowchef Foods business for a dollar, as a project to rebuild his mind.

She let out a sigh and closed the screen. How small her own life seemed. If only half of the Wiki story was true he was a remarkable man, but no less obnoxious. She hoped she'd at least landed a couple of blows on his bullying ego. She was more than a little worried about Leroy Prentice and the way she'd let him escape. In hindsight she'd done the wrong thing because that security guard and the revolting Nigel knew that's what had happened. It was just on the spur of the moment she'd let him go. She could have locked him up and gained a few brownie points from the bosses. How was a community officer supposed to balance friendship and identity with the merciless law? She was pretty certain that Max Muswell would never have understood her actions. For now there was no point in worrying. She'd lied and now that lie was her truth. Any weakness or confession, and the system would skin her alive. As a professional police officer she knew she should file a report about the workers at Meadowchef Foods. She knew that nothing would happen. The local commander was under pressure because of the rate of street robbery. The last thing he would want was a can of non-English-speaking worms tipped out on his desk. It wouldn't hurt for her to do some digging, check out who exactly delivered the labor and where they were kept when they weren't working. Tomorrow was scheduled as another afternoon shift and perhaps she'd take a look. Her first priority was sleep.

She awoke to the constant groaning of the traffic on Camberwell Road. The Number Forty red London buses trundled past day and night between Aldgate and Dulwich. Her home was a small bedsit above an empty shop. The view from her window was of a run-down taxi office and a hairdresser's salon. It was a little damp and creepy with the deserted premises underneath but it was just about affordable for a woman on her own. That expression bugged her. On her own. Yes, she was on her own. No one said she was independent, proud, resourceful, dedicated to her work. No; she was on her own. She wasn't afraid of spiders, could unblock a sink, put a hard knee into a man's groin, and cover up her loneliness with her work. And above all else, she could drive a bus. She'd spent three years of her life driving a London bus before she had joined the police. She maintained her license as a badge of pride and as a testament to her having a foot in the teeming struggle of life outside the police. More than anything, it still gave her eyes other than those of a cop through which to view humanity.

She was out of bed and away by 8 o'clock. She walked to the community center where the bus was stored. The battery was tired and she had to use jumper cables to get it running. Her mission was to collect a group of kids with learning problems from all over the area and take them to a day center. She scraped ice from the windscreen as the motor warmed up. Her mind turned to the obnoxious Max Muswell. His Rolls-Royce would be worth about a quarter of a million pounds. She'd settle for a couple of new batteries. Her first stop was at the Lomond Grove High Rise to collect Irene, her escort helper.

Her round followed the usual pattern of kids not ready, with mums begging her to wait. Others stood pinch-faced and shivering, holding their child at cold bus stops. Irene scolded and cuddled kids equally in her loud embracing manner.

"Come along, come along. You late and others wait. Sweet Jesus loves a smile."

"You're a ray of Jamaican sunshine to me," Paula yelled above the noise of kids, the belting music of Capital Radio, and the old rattly engine.

"Sun? God hides the sun to test our souls. It's easy to be happy on a sunny day."

Paula had known Irene for about four years and had built her into her own life as a kind of inner voice. Her existence was in the hands of Jesus with liberal doses of the Virgin Mary. Bad things were to test you as an individual person and good things were to be shared. There was no more and no less to life than that. Paula had no religious faith, a fact which Irene saw as an act of God.

"Jesus sent you to examine my beliefs. The more you doubt the more the Lord whispers answers in my ear. I pray to Jesus for you every day, Paula. He protects you because he's afraid of what I'd say to him if he didn't."

"I think I'd be with Jesus on that one."

They pulled into the day center car park at 9:30. Paula loved these kids and had known many of them since she'd started as a volunteer driver. A little girl named Lauren stopped as she got out, to show her a library book. It was The Incredible Mr Fox.

"Boggis eats three chickens a day," she said in a tiny voice.

"Wow, that's so greedy. You wouldn't do that would you?"

"No. I wouldn't do that."

She watched her walk away. It didn't look as if she'd ever eaten any portion of a chicken.

"Poor little mite. Her mother's expecting a new baby. Lauren may have to go into a children's home for a while if she can't cope," said Irene.

Paula sighed. There were so many sad stories around these kids, too many to focus on individual cases. In this context she wasn't a cop. She wasn't representing any vision of society, except her own sense of goodwill to others. Once she pulled on the uniform, she stood for the law and the system. Sometimes too much of her inner self spilled over into her work. Like when she'd let Leroy Prentice go.

She did some shopping for groceries, did the reverse bus run at 12:30 and just about had time to be ready for duty at 2:00 p.m. She liked her life this way. She joined the gaggle of cops in the parade room at Brixton police station.

"Why do I always think of hearts and flowers when I see you, Paula?"

She laughed as a cop ten years her junior, known as "Basher" called out to her. He was famed as a police boxer and had a certain reputation for an over-physical approach to his work.

"'Cause you're an oversexed moron," said another officer. "Paula's pledged to me, ain't ya?"

She glanced at the speaker, a pleasant-faced rounded guy who'd been widowed a couple of years back.

"I said I'd taken the pledge, Jim. You should get your ears cleaned out," she replied.

The boys laughed. In the main they were young, far younger than her. The youngest candidate for her affections had been twenty-two. He'd invited her to play on his Xbox. His enthusiasm crashed when she had to admit that she'd never played a video game.

The sergeant began to list the wanted suspects, the latest thefts, robberies and burglaries, the missing juveniles, the latest hangouts for dealers, the intelligence on who had firearms, a general memo from Scotland Yard about terror attacks with vehicles, and finally a warning from the district commander about officers not wearing their caps and helmets. Paula knew that most of the information was a waste of time. Brixton received hundreds of emergency response calls every day. Every officer fought fires for nearly all of their shift.

The door opened and a young inspector came in. He walked to the front of the room and looked at the late-shift crew. There were guys there with twenty-five years' service, guys with commendations and medals for bravery. The inspector raised his hands in a gesture for them all to stand.

"Fuck me! It's Jesus raising the fucking dead," said an old-sweat called Vic-the-nick on account of his nose for crooks.

Paula giggled and a few guys laughed aloud. The inspector lowered his hands indicating they could all sit down. This had to be a jerk. Obviously he was a college-boy entry on the accelerated promotion scheme.

"Good afternoon. I'm Inspector Crispin Bissel. I am your shift inspector for the next few months. I'm really looking forward to getting to know you and joining you on patrol."

"You wouldn't say that if you'd ever breathed in one of Basher's farts, guv," said a gruff voice.

The inspector looked a little nervous at such disrespect. He carried on his introduction.

"You'll all get to know me, I hope. I only see opportunities and challenges."

"Better mind the fucking steps, then guv," interrupted Vic-the-nick.

The crew laughed. Paula felt a shred of sympathy for the young man. He was out of his depth, but soon enough he'd be thrown a line and rescued back to Scotland Yard for further career development and promotion. All he knew was college life of essays and lectures. This was the front line and these guys faced it day after day. One of the shift was sick with a fractured skull. Another had just come back after a stab wound. Little management jargon pep talks were not the flavor at Brixton.

"Can I let this lot out to provide the public with the abuse and maltreatment they deserve?"asked the sergeant.

"Yes. Do we have PC Middleton here?"

"It's the short, beautiful one dressed up as a woman," he replied.

Inspector Bissel visibly winced at the political incorrectness. Paula smiled.

"I hear you're pretty short in some places, sarge."

"That's the last time I'll call you beautiful. If ever you want to check out my dimensions, Paula?"

"I've lost my detective's magnifying glass, sarge."

"Go on you lot, fuck off and don't dare bring me any stinking hobo fleabags for drunk and disorderly. If you have to just push them over the border into Camberwell."

The inspector had turned to a ghostly white. He'd fallen into a boiling vat of sexism and outrageous cynicism. In five minutes the foundations of his superior rank and management confidence had been washed away by a flood of reality.

"PC Middleton, I need to speak to you in my office."

"OK guv, did I get caught on CCTV with my hat crooked?"

"There's been a complaint."

Straightaway she had a good idea of what it would be.

"My conscience is clear, sir."

The inspector re-inflated himself as she used the correct term to address him. She followed him through a couple of corridors narrowed by filing cabinets and bags of riot equipment that had no proper home. He seated himself at his desk and motioned for her to sit.

"At this stage, Paula, this matter has not been elevated to Scotland Yard's complaints bureau, but it is a very serious matter."

"It's the crooked hat isn't it? It's the shape of my head, sir."

Her heart was pounding. She'd bluffed out a lot of shit over the past thirteen years and so far she'd survived.

"I believe you went to Meadowchef Foods yesterday?"

"You got me there, sir. That's true."

"A Mr Max Muswell has complained that he has received a report from his security guard."

"Don't tell me. I parked in his parking bay?"

"I must ask you not to interrupt me. This is a serious matter. He alleges that you chased a suspect who was carrying items stolen from his depot, but that you let him go."

"I saw a man running, but I didn't catch him. I did stop a guy and search him but he was clean."

"So you followed all the procedures of filling in a search form and recording all his details?"

"Nah. I'm a community cop. That means keeping things cool."

"You've no record?"

"No."

"That in itself is a serious breach of the regulations and the Police and Criminal Evidence Act code of practise."

"Look guv, I'll plead to that, OK. No contest. Stop the fight."

"If this case goes up to the Yard it could mean your suspension and dismissal."

"Wouldn't look too good on your first day, sir."

"That's impertinent, constable."

"I'm looking at you, guv, and I'm wondering whether or not to help you out or let you hang yourself."

Inspector Bissel sat back in his chair almost gasping like a landed carp. She smiled at him and softened her face. Perhaps he was a lost boy who needed a friend?

"OK, explain yourself."

"The guy I stopped was not the thief, so we can forget that, and no one can prove otherwise. Mr Muswell runs a shady business with illegal slave labor and I told him I was aware of it. He told me to fuck off and mind my own business and I told him to fuck off in equal terms. He's not a man to stand up to if you don't want a fight. He doesn't want me on his case, so he's decided to fit me up with some lies to get me off his back. He hopes you're going to fall for it. You're young and green and he'll make bullets for you to fire at your own troops."

"This is outrageous, constable. I imagine you've filed all the necessary reports detailing all your suspicions about slave labor."

"I've just filed it now, sir."

"But you did not submit an intelligence report."

"No. I went home and drank a bottle of wine instead."

"You give me no option but to pass this file up to the formal complaints bureau for investigation. We still have the option to resolve this locally."

"How?"

"You concede that you made an error and did not follow proper procedures."

"With respect, sir, you can fuck right off. Look, let's get the resources to nail this prick for exploiting those poor souls. We all know the hoods who supply them."

"Do we?"

"Look, you're as green as the fucking Serpentine Lake. The local end is the McCarthy boys. They do the delivery and enforcement for Russian thugs and I mean real murderous bastards. I mean people who cut your dick off and make you eat it."

"How do you know this?"

"We all know. Every toe-rag knows the McCarthy boys. This Max Muswell is tough and has a heart of stone, but he can't get them off his back. You, inspector, could make a name for yourself by wiping your ass with that report and getting some resources to go to war with this lot."

"To defeat the Russian Mafia, a bunch of racketeers, and a semi-celebrity billionaire business man like Max Muswell?"

"Yeah, and anyone else who pops up as a target."

"I note your comments of course, but I'm afraid I must follow complaints procedures. I hereby serve you with a copy of the complaint and ask you if you have any formal comment. You do not have to say anything but anything you do say...."

"Yeah, blah, blah, blah, sir. Last thing while I'm here. I propose to arrest the depot manager for attempting to bribe a police officer."

"How?"

"He offered me a whole sack of brussel sprouts if I might care to join him in his love nest."

Inspector Bissel avoided eye contact.

"Can you prove it?"

"Not exactly, just like they can't prove the guy I stopped was the thief. I know it and you know it."

"I order you not to arrest this man. It could look like a reprisal."

"That's fine, sir. I'll bring that up when I'm interviewed by the Complaints Bureau detectives. In the meantime, what shall I do about the hungry slaves and the Russian Mafia?"

"Constable, I can't lift the lid on something like that."

"There you are then. Max Muswell got what he wanted. Nice to talk to you, sir."

# CHAPTER 3

She was in deep shit and she knew it. Inspector Bissel was a new officer-class management clone, thinking only of self-advancement. The old days of loyalty had gone and now it was every man for himself. Soon every cop would have to wear a body camera. Every conversation would have to be recorded. Politically correct assessors would analyze every interaction for deviance. Surveillance culture robbed everyone of personality or humor. If she had her time again she'd be a heavily armed anarchist hermit. She wouldn't have had a best friend who had run off with her husband, wouldn't have waited until she was thirty-nine and on her own to long for a child. She was where she was, in the shit with a late shift ahead of her.

As a community officer she had an amount of freedom. She collected her in-tray of reports and signed out an unmarked car. She wanted to get away from the claustrophobic atmosphere of the station. She drove to Coldharbour Lane and sorted through her paperwork. She had a dozen or so people to see about stolen bikes, trouble with neighbors, kids smoking weed in the stairwells, and on and on. A couple of times she passed by Meadowchef Foods and couldn't resist parking up in the wet darkness of the evening, just to see whatever there might be to see. It was 6:30 p.m. when a scruffy Ford Transit minibus drove in through the gates. Her impression was that it was full of workers. Her guess was that this was the night shift and that the day shift would soon be coming out. She started the motor and watched as the bus emerged. By chance she was pointed the same way. She let two cars create a gap and pulled out to follow. She could see several workers inside but the windows were steamed up. One of the tail lamps wasn't working, something that could be very useful if she chose to pull in the driver. The London traffic was a slow red-and-white smear of steamy exhausts and exasperated car horns. The bus just got through an amber traffic light and she had to force her way through on red to stay in contact. So far she'd been lucky. She followed the bus north toward central London, until it turned east and headed for Peckham. She was well off her own patch and she hadn't told anyone of her mission. If anything went wrong she was well out of line. They'd entered a tangled housing estate, with blocks of older style brick-built flats. The bus stopped as she switched off her lights and held back in the darkness. She counted eighteen persons as they darted out into the block. She smiled to herself. If all else failed she could get them for overloading. The Ford Transit drove off but she'd noted the registration. For now she wanted to know where the Meadowchef workers had gone. She considered her options. She was in uniform and that could be an advantage. When in doubt she knew that fortune favored the bold. She picked up her folder of papers and walked into the block. The foreign-accented voices of the group were above her, echoing down the damp concrete steps. For sure there would be minders and maybe an actual gang-master with them. She felt alone and exposed but she'd come too far to back down. A door banged shut and the voices became muffled. They were on the third floor. She could just leave it now, file a report, leave it to the bosses. If she had a flat number she could run a voter's register check.

The front doors of the separate apartments looked out onto an open landing. The voices were coming from the furthest door. She began to walk toward it when suddenly it snapped open and a white male figure hurried in her direction. It was the big ugly form of Billy McCarthy. She immediately stopped and knocked on the first door. A light came on inside. The guy was on top of her now. She spoke to him directly.

"Excuse me, sir, there was a burglary on the ground floor this afternoon. Were you at home and did you see anything suspicious?" she said.

"Nah, can't help you," he said.

"Well, be aware then, sir. You know, there's villains about."

"Yeah, thanks."

He scampered on down the stairs. That could have been difficult. She'd only seen him once before at the station when he'd been locked up for stabbing a man in a nightclub. The door she'd knocked opened on a chain. An old woman peered at her through the gap.

"I'm looking for Mr Briggs. Do you know him?" said Paula.

"Not here."

"Thanks. Sorry to trouble you."

The door closed. She would have liked to go in and ask a couple of questions about the neighbors but she knew that could be bad news for the resident. People didn't talk about the McCarthy brothers. She strolled up to the end apartment and noted the number; 17. Through the kitchen window she could just see into a lounge covered with mattresses. Her luck had held out. Time to go home.

If she filed an honest intelligence report, Inspector Bissel would know that she'd been out of her area without consultation or permission. If he was looking for a cop to bust, she was already in the frame. The next two days were off duty. She needed a break and soon enough the complaints bureau team would be adding to her troubles. She also needed a drink. Her cellphone rang.

"Honey, is that the loveliest, sweetest, safest, smoothest bus driver in the world?"

"No, Sally Smith, it is not. You've got the wrong number."

"Right now I'm seeing the tears rolling down the cheeks of a little guy in a wheelchair 'cause he can't get to see the Christmas lights in town."

"That sounds like a lie."

"I'm seeing him in my imagination."

"You're a dangerous fantasist. Someone should call the cops before you do some harm."

"I've called you. Help me. Please?"

"It's going to cost you."

"Name your price."

"A Kentucky Fried Big Daddy and bring your own wine."

"Diet Coke?"

"Nah, full fat. I'm only eating natural products these days."

"That poor little boy has almost stopped crying."

"Tell him to stop snivelling or the driver will give him a slap."

"You're a star."

"I'm hungry. You've got about forty-five minutes. Don't forget your own wine. I can't feed your addiction as well as mine."

She no longer kept a car and travelled home on the 45 bus. She needed some company and Sally was a good person even though she was from a rather different world. She was an educated woman of about forty-five, dedicated to her life as a social worker. She dealt with areas like respite care, kids with family problems, and learning issues. Paula often watched her wince when she used words and banter from the street. She'd met her when a child had kicked off on the bus and bitten the escort. She was posh, immensely patient, and often needed a volunteer community bus driver at short notice. So far she'd never truly talked to her. Perhaps today would be the day to see inside.

It wasn't long before the finger-licking bonhomie and a Walmart bargain merlot turned the vino into veritas.

"I was so glad you called. I didn't want to just come home alone and I would have ended up in the pub with the savages. They're good guys, but you can't really talk."

"Did you want to talk?"

"Your counselling slip is showing."

"Oh dear, am I that obvious?"

"At home we just said nosey and got on with it."

"I see."

"I'm sorry, I was a bit defensive or maybe passive-aggressive."

"Maybe *I'm* nosey, so let's get on with it."

Paula laughed and poured two more glasses of wine.

"We've still got your bottle."

"I've got to drive."

"Crash on the sofa. I'm guessing you've got no one waiting at home?"

"Now *your* counselling slip is showing."

"Don't waste your chance then."

"I'm on my own, yes. Just didn't happen." Sally took a good slug of the wine. "You sort of feel ashamed, or at least I do."

"At first I felt empowered in a sort of defiant way. I felt I'd just scored a solo goal and all the crowd was cheering and patting me on the back. Then the game swept on, the noise stopped and the crowd went home."

"What happened?" asked Sally.

"I was married. I had a best friend. She screwed my husband. The good news is that so far I've not been arrested for a double murder."

"Where did you hide the bodies?"

"They're under that sofa. Sweet dreams."

"You must have felt betrayed."

"I guess that's how I felt. It was the shock, the sense of having been duped. It's not easy living with a cop, so I can see reasons. If you work different shifts you've got loneliness and opportunity. The truth is that a cop's closest family is often the work team. You go through things together you can't share at home."

"And your future?"

"Looks like I'm going up the West End to see the Christmas lights at some point. I'm fighting a formal complaint at work and to be honest I'm wondering if I care if they kick me out."

"Would you be able to help? I've got a group of kids with learning issues. I want to give them a treat and something they can do together. A lot of them haven't got transport and if we pick them up from home everyone can come. Often we do stuff and only the richer ones can join in. It's good for the parents to meet and form little support groups, just to chat, or swap tales of desperation. It can be tough on these families."

"How could I refuse that? You've damn near got me in tears."

"We've got a thirty-two seater. There's fourteen pick-ups and several with wheelchairs."

Paula blew out her cheeks.

"Well, it's a challenge."

"I know it's not a dream job. I think that's why the driver bailed out."

"Of course I'll do it."

Paula was quite astonished to find herself hugged as Sally sprang from her chair.

"I was frantic and now I'm so happy. Most of the parents will be there and I'll be there to help, or at least get in the way as a bumbling do-gooder."

"And when is this?"

"Saturday."

"Let's open the second bottle and then you tell me why a lovely woman like you never made it happen with the right guy."

"Counselling?"

"Nosey. Start with the dating website horrors. Perhaps we've dated the same monsters."

# CHAPTER 4

She looked through the list of pick-up addresses that Sally had sent her. There were several kids from her own patch on the Loughborough and Stockwell Estates in Brixton. She noted Leroy Prentice's young brother Benny was among them. There were a few around Streatham, Camberwell and one from Dulwich village. She would have to start the round quite early. She picked up the Mercedes Vario from a council yard in Tooting. Gradually the bus filled up. The vehicle was big for narrow residential streets and she needed all her skill and concentration. The kids were buzzing with excitement. Sally pushed in a CD of Christmas songs and encouraged everyone to sing. At the wheel of the big machine Paula joined in. One song was the carol "*Once in Royal David's City.*" Her mind flashed back to her own childhood at school, the nativity play and the janitor dressed up as Santa. Even her deepest cynicism couldn't hold back the simple innocence of these children's voices. She had plenty of troubles on her mind, but here in this moment she was truly happy. She found the final stop. It was a surprisingly exclusive address in Alleyn Park, Dulwich Village. The houses were grand and surely only millionaires could live there. The house had a wide front and was set back from the road. A Bentley Continental and a Rolls-Royce were on the block-paved driveway. A man was waiting outside holding the hand of boy of about ten. They boarded and found seats in the back.

"Next stop West End," she called out.

A cheer went up and the singing re-started with "Frosty the Snowman." Paula steered her little cargo of humanity through Lambeth and crossed the River Thames toward Millbank. The Houses of Parliament reflected in the water and all the city sparkled in the darkness. It didn't need much imagination to believe in the magic of Christmas. Sally came up to talk in her ear.

"So far so good. It's so beautiful."

"That last pick-up was an odd one."

"Yeah, it's not one I really know. The father's on his own and the boy needs friends and company. I think he's privately tutored, but that can't provide everything."

"Is it confidential or can you tell me what's wrong with him?"

"Sad story. Premature birth and lack of oxygen. There's a couple like that but you've got the whole catalogue of challenges back there. All the same, a song levels everyone and then raises them back up."

"Better get them singing. We're about to see the Christmas tree in Trafalgar Square."

She pushed on through the traffic to Piccadilly and Regent Street. Police security was tight in response to terrorist threats and attacks. In theory she could use the Oxford Street bus lane but it didn't surprise her when a couple of police officers stopped her, machine guns in hand.

"Red buses only," said a young severe looking constable.

"Come on, I've got a load of kids on here," Paula said.

"Move on or we'll do you for obstruction."

Paula fished in her jeans for her warrant card police ID. She handed it to the officer.

He studied it and glanced at her.

"Come on mate. It's all about community relations, you know all that shit."

"Go on then. If I'm wrong and you run down pedestrians, or you're a bomb, I might as well put this gun to my head. You know that don't you?"

"I know that."

She leaned out the window and kissed his cheek. He blushed and smiled.

"I think you're the loveliest woman who's ever kissed me."

"I think you're the loveliest copper I've ever kissed."

He waved her through. What she'd said was true. He was the first copper she'd ever kissed. She noted his shoulder service number. He was sure to get a Christmas card with her thanks.

She crawled among the buses along Oxford Street. It felt great to be V.I.P.s. At last she arrived at Marble Arch and squeezed the bus into the stop zone that she'd used so many times, as a London driver on the 73 Service.

"If anyone wants to take a stroll back to get some photos of the Oxford Street lights you'll find me here. Don't worry if you can't see me, I might have to do a circuit if they move me on. Thirty minutes max, OK?"

She pressed the button to open the doors and the bus emptied out. She hit the handbrake and went to the back to help with the tail lift for the wheelchairs. She was aware of a couple of figures standing close behind her. She stood and swivelled round.

"That was some master stroke to get this thing up Oxford Street and get parked here. Thanks for that," said a male voice.

In front of her was a tough-looking big man, his arm around the shoulder of a boy wearing a wide innocent grin on his face.

"No worries, I used to be a London bus driver."

"What? Someone like you?"

"What do you mean?"

"I can't just say it, someone like, kind and lovely."

"I'm not sure if that's sexism or bus driverism."

The guy started to laugh.

"Do I know you?"

"Did you ever catch the 73 service Oxford Circus to Stoke Newington?"

"No."

"Did I ever put you in jail?"

"What?"

"I'm a cop in my day job."

For a moment he stared at her as she stared back.

"I just don't fucking believe it," he said.

"That's just what I was thinking."

"I didn't recognize you with clothes on. I didn't mean, you know, like that way. Why do we always meet in the dark in a heap of diesel engines?"

"Must be heaven's plan."

The guy looked around him. He seemed oddly awkward and uncertain.

"This is my boy, Justin."

"Lovely to meet you Justin. I'm Paula."

She looked back to the man.

"I can't swear in front of your lad, but you can probably guess my feelings, Mr Muswell. I wasn't expecting to meet you tonight."

"All that's behind us. Please, please, Paula, we can wipe everything clean and start from here."

"I don't think we can."

"We can. Please. Look I'm going to pop over to get a shot of the lights. Drop us off last and we'll talk, OK? Please?"

She nodded agreement. It made sense to drop him last and go home to Camberwell in the bus. The situation was perplexing. He seemed like a different man, like a father, like a caring human being. All the rules around complaints against police prohibited contact with the complainant. Her career could end sooner than she thought. On the other hand, she might advance her enquiries into his labor force and his relationship with the McCarthy brothers. And on another hand all together, she might spend some time with a man who had the balls to put his fingers up to the system and carve a life from his own strength and desires. She couldn't deny to herself the attractiveness of such a man. There was goodness in him and that was never a bad place to start.

When everyone was reloaded she pulled away, this time running down to Hyde Park Corner and taking Piccadilly down to the Circus. As they were rolling down Whitehall toward Westminster she noticed Max Muswell standing up just behind her and addressing the other passengers.

"Right, Listen. Anyone want a McDonald's?"

All the kids bellowed approval. Paula glanced back at Sally, knowing she would be having the same thoughts. Many of the parents just wouldn't have the money. Mr Muswell was something of a bull in a china shop and certainly a bull.

"That's fantastic. Meadowchef Foods will treat everyone as a Christmas commercial promotion so have whatever you want. The taxman will pay. I'll come round with a list for orders. Driver, can you find a big yellow M on your way home?"

So, he'd just taken over the show. The bus would be a mess and she'd spend half the night cleaning it up. All the same he meant well and the kids would love it. She opted to get out of Central London and headed for the Elephant and Castle. She stopped outside the McD in Walworth Road.

"That's everyone except our driver," he said, as he stepped down onto the sidewalk.

"Big Tasty meal. Full fat Coke, please," she said.

"That's it. God, I love a woman who doesn't mess about and gets stuck into a bit of grub."

"And they say romance is dead," she replied.

"Ketchup?"

"Loads."

He held her eyes with a quick appraising sweep of her face. His expression was tough but with an edge of good humor. Even though he seemed to cast himself as Mr Big he was happy to go to stand in line with a huge order. Also he was happy to pay.

She watched him walk in. He was broad and moved in a way that made a few youths blocking the entrance step smartly aside. You just knew you wouldn't want to see him angry.

She looked to her side to see Melissa Prentice.

"Paula, I didn't know who he was, that Mr Muswell."

She could see some sort of anguish in her face. She was a good, strangely optimistic and innocent woman. She was blessed with a degree of simplicity that had left her open to abuse. Both her partners had disappeared back into the scenery and she'd been abandoned with two boys. Leroy was a petty criminal on the edge of the gangs and Benny had learning issues.

"I was talking to him about you. He seemed so keen to know why you were driving the bus, and all about you."

"I hope you told him I was the best cop in Brixton."

Melissa hesitated.

"I told him about Leroy. I told him you let him go. I wanted to say you were kind."

Paula looked back into her open troubled face. Now she was in the shit.

"When he said the treat was on Meadowchef Foods I realized I might have done wrong. I'm so sorry."

"No problem, Melissa. He's a kind man I think."

The woman seemed relieved and went back to her seat. Inwardly Paula was horrified. That one moment of weakness, or kindness, or mercy, or dereliction of duty just kept on haunting her. She seemed caught up in a whirlpool of coincidences that was about to drag her under. Perhaps he wouldn't put two and two together and realize that Leroy was the guy who'd run away. He seemed a man very much on top of every game. She wasn't finished by any means. His labor force was his weak point and he knew that she knew. Since her expedition to Peckham she knew a little more. There was likely to be a fight ahead, but her greatest enemy was probably Inspector Bissel. He was a young guy on the way up, and old sweat constables were not the modern police flavor.

Sally directed the singing while they waited. At last Max Muswell returned with a large cardboard box and distributed all the meals. She pulled away, the aroma of food heavy in the air and causing her stomach to rumble.

"You don't want to wait until it's cold," he said appearing at her side with her meal.

"I'll grab a bite each time we stop."

"Have a drink of your Coke."

He popped the straw into the cap and held it while she took a sip.

"That's kind but against all the rules, so that's the first and last for now."

"I wouldn't encourage you to break the regulations, officer."

She could hear a smile in his voice, but kept her eyes on the road. This situation was more than a little bizarre.

One by one she dropped off the passengers until only Sally, Max, and his son remained. In her mirror she could see a scene of cardboard and plastic devastation. The windows had been smeared by greasy fingers, ketchup and dill pickles littered the floor and seats. It was 11:00 p.m. and she wouldn't be home until midnight. In the morning she'd have to clean the bus and take it back to its yard in Tooting. She dropped Sally at her home in Herne Hill and headed for Dulwich.

"You're an ace at driving this thing."

Max and Justin had seated themselves behind her.

"Thank you."

"Don't worry about this mess, I'll get this cleared and like new in the morning. I'll get a couple of real good blokes to sort it out."

"How are they going to do that?"

"They'll turn up and fix it."

"They don't know where the bus will be."

"That's police training for you. I hadn't thought of that 'cause I assumed you'd tell me."

She thought hard. Did she really want any more to do with him? The offer of some help was tempting and since her shift started at 2:00 p.m. she wouldn't have too much time.

"Are these straight up men?"

"I'll send a couple of real pros. It's the same fellas who clean my Rolls-Royce."

She pulled up outside his house. She operated the doors.

"I'll park the bus at the Camberwell Community Center. What time can you send your guys?"

"Nine-thirty on the dot."

"Nice to meet you, Justin. Did you like the Christmas lights?" she asked the lad.

"Yeah, I'm getting an iPhone X for Christmas."

"You're a lucky man."

He beamed at her and reached out for her hand. She took it.

"Dad said you're a very pretty lady."

She looked past him to where Max was waiting just outside the bus. For once he wasn't fixing her with his searching expression.

"Was he wearing his glasses?"

"No."

"That explains it then."

"He said I could tell you."

"Your dad's a bit sneaky."

"Yeah. He hides my iPad when it's meal times."

"Come on, Justin. Busy day tomorrow," said Max.

"He doesn't wear glasses," Justin added.

Paula chuckled as she closed the doors. She watched them as they walked up to the house, his arm around the boy's shoulders. Doubtless he was a bruising bastard to deal with but in this moment there was something touching about his unconditional love for the young man. Was this the child that his wife had left him with? Was this the kid he hadn't fathered? Guessing Max Muswell's character, he didn't seem the sort of man to care for such a child. For sure she was never going to know what sort of man he was. With a bit of luck she'd never see him again.

# CHAPTER 5

This was no way to spend a Sunday morning. A wave of stale-food gas spilled out for her to breathe as she opened the doors of the bus. She'd brought a plastic sack for the trash and started to pick up the packaging. She doubted Max Muswell's men would show. It wasn't yet nine-thirty and in any event there was nowhere to plug in a vacuum cleaner. To clean the windows would take at least an hour. She heard a vehicle pull up and looked out. All she could see was a deep-blue Bentley Continental. Max got out and went to the trunk where he found a rechargeable hoover and a bucket overflowing with polishes and aerosol cans. He handed the bucket to Justin and climbed on board.

"Morning."

"Where's the two ace car cleaners?"

"This is it. You're looking at them."

"You said you'd send the guys who do your Rolls-Royce."

"Exactly. Did you think I'd let some monkeys with a bit of dirty rag get near my cars?"

"You clean your own cars?"

"Yeah, and we do our own teeth, wash our own clothes, and do our own shopping."

"I'm impressed."

"If ever you want to help with the shopping you're welcome. I've had a lot of unexpected trouble in the bagging area."

She stared at him. Did he remember that he'd filed a complaint against her? Had it registered that she'd lied about Leroy Prentice? She would be in ocean-deep shit if the complaints bureau caught her talking to him. Yet, here she was chatting to him while he helped her clean the bus. He'd already begun a vigorous attack with the vac while Justin diligently polished the windows. Somewhere, bouncing between the front and the back of her mind was the fact that he'd told his son she was pretty. Then he'd clearly manipulated a situation so that the lad could tell her. She found a surface cleaner spray and worked on the handrails. She couldn't stop herself taking a few long looks at him. He was strong and powerful. His thick forearms flexed and rippled as he worked. His neck had an aspect of tree trunk and his pale blue T-shirt was tight across his pecs. He took a couple of calls on his cellphone. His manner was curt and decisive. He didn't raise his voice but seemed to ram the words like fists into the ear of the other party.

"Well done, son, but you've missed a bit back there," he said to his boy.

Justin scampered back and perfected his work.

Should she raise any of their mutual issues? Should she raise the plight of the unfortunate wretches who worked at Meadowchef foods? This was a matter of humanity as much as it was police business. The questions kept churning in her mind.

"Right then, Paula. Job looks good to me. I believe you have to drive the bus over to Tooting? I'll follow you in the Bentley and drop you back home. Or, if you're not busy it's a lovely day and I fancy a stroll along the beach at Brighton. We could all nip down there for the afternoon."

Was this an invitation to a date or what? Obviously he would include his son.

"I'm on duty at two."

"I bet you could get off if you wanted to."

"If I wanted to."

His eyes scrutinized hers. Desperately she tried to hide the inescapable truth. She did want to. The police owed her several missed rest days on account of extra duties following recent terrorist attacks in London. It was a Sunday so she had no specific appointments. She could call in and see how they were fixed for staff and use one of her days. If she wanted to.

"Max...."

"Paula...."

"I'm not supposed to talk to you. You've filed a complaint against me."

"That's all in the past. That's all over."

"It's not that simple. I've been served with a formal notice and the system grinds on."

"Nah, I've already called a guy. It's in the trash. The guard was wrong and Meadowchef has signed an apology."

Paula felt as if her mouth had dropped open.

"Apology? What, you? You wouldn't eat humble pie if it was the last morsel in the world."

"A man's got to do what a man's got to do."

"Who did you call?"

"Ghostbusters of course."

She suppressed a giggle.

"But I know you spoke to Melissa Prentice."

"Who?" he answered with a wink.

"OK, Max, here's the deal breaker. As a human being I'm concerned about those poor sods working in your depot. Forget the cops and the immigration authorities. I'm talking about me as a woman. If they're on the table for conversation, I'll come with you."

"Nothing's off the table, but not this afternoon. Justin needs a bit of air out of London."

"When will you talk?"

"When you come out for dinner on Tuesday."

"Is that an offer of a date?"

"I guess it must be. I'm a bit out of practice."

"It won't be the sort of place to talk about the McCarthy brothers."

"So you know the shape of the problem? Great minds think alike. I'll cook some Thai fish soup with jasmine rice."

"At your place?"

"Yeah, I've got a cooker and everything."

She pulled out her cell and called the duty officer at the station. It was fixed. She was free.

"Is this the worst mistake I'm ever going to make?"

"That depends on how I cook the rice. Long grain is so much easier, but I hate to chicken out of things."

This man confused her. He was strong and proud, but could admit to error. He was generous and kind, yet he exploited poor powerless people. There was a dangerous element to his personality, but she felt safe in his company. He didn't have that coiled spring of violence in him that she could always sense in unpredictable psycho-types. On the other hand he had an anger that paced up and down like a caged lion behind his intense eyes. More confusing than him was the surge she felt in herself. She hated to admit it but his proximity alone made her aware of her body, her breasts, and her sex. On the bus last night when he'd been behind her she'd become a little damp and OK, she'd thought about him when she'd soothed her tensions and loneliness at dawn. Even worse, he wanted her. She could feel his sexual power when he looked at her, as if he could just will her to give way to him. She was equally fearful and thrilled about what he might unleash in her.

"OK, driver. Take me to Brighton via Tooting."

Without warning he leaned in and kissed her cheek.

"Thanks, Paula."

"If you were a government minister I could run to the papers now and get you busted."

"Not if you kiss me back."

"I could lie."

"You've got form for that I must admit."

"Oh, all right then," she said as she pecked his cheek. "That's for getting all the kids a meal last night and having the good manners to help me clean up."

"This is the best Sunday morning I've had for years, maybe ever."

She smiled at him and didn't say she didn't feel the same way.

# CHAPTER 6

The Brighton sea air was cold but bright. She felt guilty for being there, being free in somehow stolen hours with a man she shouldn't be with. Justin had taken her hand as they'd thrown pebbles into the waves beating onto the shore. He looked like any other young man but she guessed his mental age was about six or seven, from what she knew of other kids she carried on the bus with Irene. She wanted to find out more but didn't want to talk in front of the boy. They strolled up the pier and watched while he played arcade games. Then Max took her hand. Like they were an item, like that was how she was beginning to feel. She'd invited him to take it with a quick glance and a smile but of course she could deny that to herself if she wanted to. If she wanted to. He squeezed it with a firm gentleness a couple of times to signal an understanding and a thanks. How could she know that? How could she have tuned to a man by a banal moment holding his hand. This man was a bastard. She was a lonely woman heading for forty-two. It was obvious she was just like a stupid kid believing that Santa came and that you could fall in love. Naive lonely people were always gulled in by crooks. A cop like her would see it straightaway wouldn't she? Her marriage had ended four years ago but it wasn't until a few days ago that she'd felt exposed and alone. Her heart had re-opened but so had the box of fear and insecurity. If only he would take her in his arms and hold her. If only she could walk away back to her manageable life.

And then the bastard did it. He pulled her round to face him and held her. No sexual lunge or forced kiss but a hug, a cry out to another person, a cry out to be held and validated as a someone to somebody. Wordlessly he clung to her as she clung to him letting her joy and fear sob onto his shoulder. His hand was stroking her dark, bobbed hair. This bastard was taking her and just at this moment she couldn't stop him. She'd kill anyone who tried to stop her living this emotion. He held her away for a moment, searching her wet eyes.

"Maybe I should be sorry to make you cry," he said.

"It's not you. It was happiness."

"Then it must have been me who made you happy."

This time she herself pulled him back and his truly powerful arms brought her close to him and wrapped around her.

"What's happening here?" he asked in a deep voice as his cheek pressed against the top of her head.

"I'll take the fifth. No one has to incriminate themselves."

"I'm so happy you came today. That night at the yard wasn't good. Look, I don't like the police. I was angry you'd let that guy get away and I was angry you'd stood up to me."

"'Cause I'm a woman?"

"I'm going to be honest and say yes to that. Yes, I'm that sort of man. A man has fear of me. What can I do with a lovely woman?"

"You can liberate those poor people who work for you."

"I wanted to talk about you and me today, but I saw yesterday you truly care about others. We'll talk fully on Tuesday. It's not a simple issue."

"I do know that."

"If you kick over a basket of poisonous snakes you can't afford a single one to be left."

"We'll talk," she said into his chest.

Justin had come back. Max took one of his hands and Paula took the other. They ambled back along the promenade in the dusk of a winter's evening. It sure felt like happiness.

"Can you come for a quick drink before I drop you home?" he asked.

They were on the edge of London. She'd so much enjoyed being with him and Justin that she really didn't want to go home. All the same she wanted to keep a line drawn.

It would be a mistake to agree to it.

"Yeah, I'd love to, thanks."

He glanced across at her. The Bentley was wide and while he was driving he kept his eyes on the road. For a civilian he drove well. He exuded a competence. He would always be the guy to take command in a crisis."

"We've got a rabbit," said Justin

"I hope you're going to show me."

"He eats the doormat."

"And the table legs and the door," added Max, laughing.

"He's naughty."

"He's a rabbit," she commented.

The house was luxurious but unfussy. For sure it was no show home, with scattered toys and the untidiness of family life. There was the predictable huge TV, the marble work-topped kitchen with fancy island, the large dining room with posh chairs. Max busied himself with fixing a meal for Justin.

"I'll get him off to bed and we can relax for a minute," he said.

She raised an eyebrow. Well, she'd put her head in the lion's mouth. The problem was that she was more afraid of her own potential than of his. The lad hugged her as he said goodnight. Maybe his whole life would unfold with his present innocence? Puberty would change him and the world out there placed little value on open simplicity. At last, Max handed her a single malt whisky with ice. He cleared a space from clutter and joined her on the sofa, sipping a Coke. He lay back his head and sighed.

"Where are we now, where are we now?" he sang in a Bowie imitation.

"That's not a bad question, Max."

"I guess you want to talk about the workers at Meadowchef?"

"I do, but not exclusively."

He turned to her with a look in his eye that held her, wanted her. He reached out and stroked her cheek. She leaned her head into his large strong hand. The power of him took away her own will, like that moment before sleep. She felt his lips. Oh God, the feel of his lips, the warmth and tenderness of his touch. He stroked along her jawline and drew her in with an overwhelming gentleness. Could she ever open her eyes? The more she left them closed, the more he would know his power to control her. Deep inside her she was warmed by a physical response, but she didn't want that distraction. Her own lips searched to know the landscape of this man. She guessed he was watching her, gaining that prize of her compliance and need. She peeked out to find him closed in his own world of her, drawing a joy from her. She ran her hand back across his cropped hair. The feel of fur thrilled her, almost jolted a sense of urgency to feel his flesh, to possess his body. As he moved away he was smiling, never losing the hold of her eyes.

"Oh dear," she said.

"Oh dear indeed, my dear."

"Where are we now, where are we now?"

He let out a long sigh.

"I don't know, but I do know where I'm going to be."

"Where?"

"I'm going to be taking you home."

"Did I fail the kiss test?"

"You failed the temptation test. I'm the opposite sex you see. No woman has the right to do that to a man."

"It was an accident. I didn't mean to."

"A first kiss is so sad because there can never be another one. I want to keep this last moment just as a sealed thing inside myself. I don't want to lose it in a hundred kisses."

She studied him. She understood him completely. She'd taken him for a brute and a bully albeit a sexy, desirable one. Now what was she dealing with?

"When would you like the next ninety-nine?"

"Just keep them warm for Tuesday, unless my conduct has put you off."

"I'm not sure if you're a perfect gentleman or a perfect con man playing a longer game."

"Either way I'm perfect then."

"Thanks for today. I needed, well, I needed a break."

"Was that all you needed?"

"Look, Max, I don't know you and you've stormed into my life and if I started, you'd have a whole box of stuff tipped out on this floor."

"And just look at the state of the place already."

"Take me home before I double park in your first kiss space."

He lowered his eyes, stood up, and stroked her hair. He was so right not to push further. She'd not met any man like this before. If he'd touched or held her, she would have had no resistance.

"How can you leave Justin to drive me home?"

"There's a self-contained annex and I have a housekeeper. I know the place is a mess but I like it to be a home. When I'm away on business or at the stables, things get kind of womanized. Justin's not too tidy and we man out together."

"You love him so much, don't you?"

"Sure. I'm guessing you know some of my history?"

"Max, I did read your Wiki entry."

"It's not too far off the whole truth. Yes, he was born to my ex-wife. We'd tried for a baby you know. This is where you put the obvious question."

She knew what that question would be. Was there DNA proof of parentage?

"If you know the question, what's the answer?"

"The answer is that he was born to my ex-wife. She'd been a woman I'd loved. I don't love her now but that boy is like that kiss we just had. He came from a particular context of time and there he's fixed. You might have kissed me wishing it was some other man. I might have kissed you wanting just to get you to bed. You know we can all look up at the stars and tear apart any meaning to this tiny life on this little planet. But a helpless babe looking up at you is a universe and a betrayal is a fucking super nova explosion to break your heart. I walked away from that episode of my life with some love still in my soul. I left the bitterness to the lawyers and no, I've never done a DNA test."

She couldn't answer him. Tears burned behind her eyes. He was so wise, so different from the man she'd first met. She pulled him to her in a way that she'd never handled a man. He felt so strong, so tireless and hard. She wasn't ready to intrude into his emotions. She sensed a swirl of pride, ambition, and dominance in his psyche.

Although he could think reflectively she was sure he could lash out in passion and you might not want to be there.

"Max, thanks so much for letting me inside like that."

"It's nothing. I can get real boring. You can't leave me wallowing in my own selfish mess. Give me somewhere to start to unravel your ball of string?"

"I had a husband and a best friend. Now they're an item and I'm not."

"Easy solution. Fall in love with your best friend and marry them."

"She was a girl."

"Times have changed. Anyone can be anything."

"Not me."

"So how did it leave you feeling?"

She was still holding him. She sighed and he seemed to sense her soft abandon into him. He pulled her to his chest and again he stroked her hair.

"It left me feeling ashamed. Shame is when you put yourself in others' eyes and know how they're seeing you. You kind of live in that other-mindedness that you fucked up and everyone knows it. That feeling hardens like a jagged broken bone heals, you don't want to move it. Everyone pats your back and one day all the doctors go away and you're alone."

"And now?"

"That's where I've stayed. You get used to not poking the wound. Your system closes down. You allow yourself anger because that's respectable. The loneliness hardens into a shame, like that no one wanted you. Max, I'm not making sense. I'd never talk like this, making me sound like some sort of desperate psycho bitch."

Still he held her.

"Thanks for letting me inside like that."

His voice was deep and vibrated into her cheek

"We kind of started in the deep end didn't we?"

"Always swim up toward the light. I'll hold your hand, if you'll hold mine," he said.

# CHAPTER 7

The note in her in-tray asking her to report to Inspector Bissel probably wouldn't be good news. She'd done the early bus run for the day center kids with Irene and come directly to work. She knew she was in a daze, a delicious confusion by the name of Max. She knocked on the office door.

"Come."

"You want to see me, guv?"

"PC Middleton, yes. Sit down."

His face was spotty and pale. His shoulders were narrow and droopy, his white neck long and thin with an Adam's apple like an elevator in a high rise block. His hands looked soft and almost feminine. She tried to adopt an expression of formal neutrality.

"Two things. I've had a memo from the complaints bureau. For some reason they've asked me to withdraw your official notice of investigation."

"For some reason, like what sort of reason?"

"What?"

"I've been doing this a lot longer than you, sir. Complaints bureau don't vaguely withdraw a complaint. There will be a reason and I want to know it."

He sighed with an ill-concealed impatience and leafed through the file.

"The complainant has made a statement saying that he was misinformed by one of his staff and your actions were correct."

"Well, that's some pretty clear sort of reason."

The inspector drew his thin lips into a grimace which she imagined could be a smile.

"And now there's an even bigger problem."

"Not the crooked hat again? I've told you it's the shape of my head."

He ignored her response and let out an effeminate whinny.

"On Wednesday you signed out a detective pool car."

"Guilty."

"That vehicle was flashed by an enforcement camera in Peckham, for running a red light at forty-six miles per hour in a thirty zone."

Shit. Now she had to think fast. She remembered running the light chasing the bus carrying the Meadowchef workers. She was out of her area and hadn't notified anyone. With most bosses she could tell the truth and that would be the end of it. This guy was out to bust cops to prove his politically correct credentials. She needed to play for time.

"There'll be a photograph and a printout of the camera calibration in that case."

"Of course. What were you doing there and why did you break the law to the danger of other road users?"

"May I offer you some advice on the application of the law, sir?"

"I don't think I need that from you, constable."

"Well, take some advice from one her majesty's citizens accused of a crime. You have questioned me about an alleged offence without issuing me with the notification of my rights. On this occasion I can overlook that and not file a report."

"You are impertinent."

"Impertinent and completely right, sir."

The young inspector flicked through the papers spread in front of him. Even now she had some sympathy with him. If he didn't wise up, his life was going to be struggle.

"That's it for now, constable. I'll get back to you. In the meantime, your driving permit is suspended."

"Happy Christmas, guv," she said as she closed the door.

She walked along the corridor, her head down.

"Can't be that bad, Paula?"

She raised her eyes to see Superintendent Jack Miller, head of the detective department. She'd worked with him on several serious cases, the last one being a baby battered by the mum's new boyfriend.

She'd been credited with getting the mother to give evidence against him.

"Things could be better, guv."

"Let's get a coffee. I owe you a least a bottle of scotch for that last job."

"Can I drink it now?"

"This ain't like you."

"What am I like then, guv?"

"Blimey, you're my favorite community officer with a heart of gold. You could still be a detective if you wanted that."

He was a kind man from the old school. He defended his troops even when they'd overstepped the mark. His face was reddened with broken veins perhaps reflecting his own love of a wee sip of whisky.

"Thanks, but I'll stick to what I know."

"Coffee. Don't go all bloody purist-vegan and ask for a decaf latte with soya milk. This is Brixton."

"Strong black. This sure is Brixton, guv."

"I think that might be non-PC. Thank God I haven't got too long to serve."

She sat in the corner of the canteen while he got the drinks. She knew that he could solve all her issues but it wasn't her style to go upstairs with a problem. He settled back to face her.

"I've been having a little look at the McCarthy brothers."

The old detective's expression changed to one of alert intensity.

"Someone needs to skin those bastards. Tell me what you know."

"They're supplying workers to businesses. I don't know the details but my guess is that they're all illegals without papers."

"Modern slavery. The old-fashioned variety never ended, really."

"I don't know where they get them, but I've heard it's Russian Mafia types."

"Don't get your pretty head blown off, Paula."

She studied his face. She was certain he wouldn't want this problem. Street robbery was the absolute priority. The commissioner had been dragged in front of a parliamentary committee to explain why such offences were escalating. The answer was simple; resources had been moved to twenty-years-out-of-date celebrity sexual offences and everyday modern counter- terrorism.

"I've got an address in Peckham where they keep a mob of these poor sods. The McCarthy boys run the show locally. They approach a business and tell the boss he has to take their labor force. If they don't cooperate, bad things can happen to the premises or the man himself."

"It's a perfect business model."

"A lot of these jobs are low paid anyway so it's hard to find workers. No one can live in London on a normal wage."

"Paula, I hate the McCarthy boys to the depth of my soul. They swagger around South London and everyone lives in terror of them. The Russians add a massive element. It's like throwing a stone at an aircraft carrier and I haven't even got a stone."

"What about those men living ten to a room while these thugs steal all their wages?"

"You're a lovely caring woman, Paula. Do you still do that community bus stuff?"

"Yeah."

"I know those guys are humans like us. They're bound to be illegals so more than likely they'll be deported. Some of them may be on the run from police back home and any life here is better than jail in Azerbaijan or wherever. I know what you're saying, but we could bust our balls on something like this and not even get a conviction."

"What about the PR side to it? I don't want to be cynical, but it's Christmas. Getting those guys a decent dinner would be fabulous TV. The commissioner might buy it on that basis."

Jack Miller leaned back and let out a long breath.

"You know you just could be so, so right. Caring cops bring the gift of freedom for Christmas."

"Are we sad, bad people, guv?"

"Yes, we have to play the media game."

"You could dress up as Santa and Inspector Bissel could be a little elf."

He looked to heaven.

"You know, Paula, I look at some cops these days and I wonder how the fuck we're going to stand up to those evil bastards out there. Inspector Bissel could carry a little seaside spade to pick up the reindeer shit."

"You shouldn't say that."

"No, you're right, but there you go. Now, from this minute you're seconded to me. Let's find out where the McCarthy boys are hanging out and all the addresses they use. Let's find out where they're using their slaves. Let's see how they're working with Russians. I'm at Scotland Yard this afternoon and I'll bend a couple of ears. If I can, I'll get you a bit of backup. Sign yourself out a pool car."

"Problem there, guv. My police driving permit is suspended. I got flashed on a red light following the McCarthy's bus a few nights ago. I had to go for it or I'd have lost them."

"Who's got the camera ticket?"

"Inspector Bissel."

"Forget it. That's shredded. I'll enjoy advising him on how to do it if he can't figure it out for himself"

"Where do I start?"

"I'd get all the latest intelligence on the McCarthys and then identify their home addresses. Don't leave the office. For the rest of today this is a desk job. Write me a report on everything you know so far and get it to me by one-thirty."

"Thanks, guv. I really needed someone on my side."

"Paula, this is a strange old job these days. We should all be on the same side. When we put up the mistletoe in the office, wait about underneath and I'll allow you to express your gratitude."

"That's an inappropriate sexist remark but I'll look forward to that, guv."

"And I still owe you a bottle of scotch. Now, get writing."

She found a desk and hammered out her report. Every minute her mind turned to Max Muswell. How would her new assignment sit alongside her relationship with him? He was right in the mix, a fact that her report failed to mention. Would it compromise her police work to discuss it with him? She had a whole day before she saw him again. A whole day. God, she'd turned into a bloody kid again. His touch and his kiss played and replayed in a loop of happiness, desire, and fear. Yes, fear was the biggest one. Fear of falling helplessly in love, fear of his underlying unknown nature, simply a fear of being a stupid foolish woman desperately wanting a man because he'd shown her attention. She'd interviewed so many streetwise folks who had believed they could never fall for a scam. And yet. And yet she longed for him, a man she had only met a couple of times. In her marriage she'd never been that bothered by sex. She'd never taken the lead, in fact would have been embarrassed. With this man she could get wet at the sound of his voice. She could pull off his clothes and grip his cock to make him want to be inside her, ruthlessly holding her open and fucking her.

"Dolly daydream you are. You in love or something?"

She snapped back to the present, to find Jack Miller smiling in front of her. Oh God, she was wet. She'd been squeezing her legs together under the desk to tease the pleasure out of her sex.

"Just making sure I hadn't forgotten anything."

"Top job, Paula. I'll speak to you in the morning. I'm going to see who's looking at people-trafficking and who's looking at Russians. There's still a couple of real cops at the top. The smart kids will love the PR angle with a bit of luck. Oh, by the way, that ticket is shredded. I gave your inspector a bit of operational advice."

For now she'd done what she could. If she wanted to she could finish her day and go home. Her cell was ringing.

"Paula, it's Max."

Her heart pounded. It was his voice. It was that man.

"Hi Max, it's Paula."

"I had the boys come round earlier to discuss the situation of my labor force. I told them to fuck off and one of the McCarthy boys has gone home to mummy crying with a split lip. Justin went to the park this afternoon and my housekeeper Rachel tells me that a blacked-out Range Rover followed them home. I'm just giving you this little bit of intelligence as a concerned citizen."

"Fucking hell, Max. We do need to talk."

"I'm getting Justin and Rachel out of here. They're already on their way to Manchester with a couple of suitably equipped guardians. The McCarthys are local pond-life and they've got no network outside of London. I'm going to be a lonely old fella watching TV tonight with a takeout pizza."

"I'm not even going to try to imagine what a suitably equipped guardian is."

"Best not think about it. Other than this load of trash, I've been thinking about you, wondering if I can hang on until tomorrow. I don't think I can."

"What about my Thai fish soup?"

"I'll stop by the Thames and catch something fresh."

"How could a girl refuse?"

"I'll pick you up at seven."

"You do that Max, and stay safe."

She clicked off. A wave of excitement swept down through her belly. Was she expected to take a bottle of wine? Or a toothbrush? Best take both just in case.

# CHAPTER 8

For a man who'd just punched one of the most brutal gangsters in London, Max looked pretty cool. He wore a blue shirt, a mid-gray striped jacket and dark pants. He was newly shaven and carried a hint of cologne. She'd gone down the stairs to meet him at the street door rather than let him in to see her humble home. She'd chosen to wear a wrap front midi dress in navy metallic with silver-heeled strappy sandals.

"Hey, do you know a girl called Paula who lives here? She's beautiful, but she's not in your league."

"She got held up at work so I said I'd stand in."

"She was cute, but you're breathtaking. When you see her, just don't mention I said anything."

She wanted at least to kiss his cheek. He put his hand to the small of her back and guided her toward the Rolls Royce which he'd left parked outside causing a traffic block. Max wasn't the sort of man to bother about parking regulations. She was torn between talking personal and talking business.

"So, you've given one of the McCarthy boys a smack in the gob?"

"I thought that other girl was still at work."

"She's working here, Max. How do you think it's going to play out? These guys can't lose face. Their whole business model is based on front and terror. If someone like you bangs one of them in the face and gets away with it everyone can see they're just bullies."

He took a deep breath.

"You're right and I know that's not the end of it. My weakness has always been Justin. These parasite shits don't scare me but if something happens to me, he's got no one. To be frank I'd kill the bastards and sit down for my dinner without a second thought."

"I don't want to hear that."

"Of course you don't. I can't believe I'm dating a cop."

"Are you dating me?"

"I hope you'd only look like that if it was a date. You couldn't walk about like that without some serious protection."

This was so wrong and it was just so right. This man was a dangerous enemy but to be on the inside was to feel utterly protected. How could she admire a man who would break the law without a second thought? She studied his face in profile. She hadn't yet asked about the scar on his cheek. His nose had suffered from his unlicensed fighting youth. His jaw was heavy and strong like a steel bridge is strong. He was forty-eight years old but had the movement and physicality of a far younger man. But where did they go from here?

"They'll be back won't they?"

"Sure. It's not a simple problem. That business needs manpower and the work is low-paid shit. It's tough to find people so the McCarthy boys fill a need. They made a mistake by trying to bully me."

"Don't you care about the poor sods they exploit?"

"If I think about it I do care, but I can't change the world, Paula. I pay minimum wage rates. The McCarthy agency pays the workers. They've got no papers. They can't walk in the job center and get an application form to be a cop, or a forklift driver."

"And if the police scooped them all up, many of them would be deported," she added, knowing the frustration of the whole situation.

"Exactly, and I'd have no work force. They're desperate people and they work hard. They steal 'cause they're hungry and I've never really bothered about that."

"Your manager, Nigel, seemed to worry."

"Yeah, he made his own decision to call in the cops. There's plenty of thieves on the estate. I'd been getting on his back because of stock losses, so I can't blame him too much. Anyway, something wonderful came out of it and I'm looking at her."

"Max, I'm glad he called me too."

He fired a kind-eyed glance at her.

"That makes me really happy to hear that. Thank you."

What a strange man. His tone was humble and innocent. He was the sort of man who could beguile a woman if he chose to. Yet he treated her with a respectful gratitude as if she were a prize he hadn't deserved to win. She thought back to his sealing of that first kiss, not wanting to weaken it with others. He'd been so right. Those feelings, that sheer joy would always be framed as a picture on a plain wall in her mind. Max Muswell was a brute, but a noble and loving one. She needed to stick to business. Once they were out of the car at his house, well, anything could happen.

"I'm going to be open with you, Max. The chief has asked me to work on the McCarthy boys. We're looking to get them locked up for a good stretch. I need your help, but I've not told my bosses that we're, you know, whatever we are."

"Looks like we're partners in crime then."

"You'd work with the police? I mean work within the law and give evidence?"

"For you, yes. For Justin, yes. Those animals made a mistake putting frighteners on me, I can tell you. All I'll say is that I'll play to win. If they pop up in my face they know what to expect."

"Max, these are armed crooks. I'm guessing you don't have a shooter?"

"Do I seem like the sort of man to keep a sawed-off shotgun and a commando knife close to hand?"

She knew he seemed exactly that kind of man.

"You seem like a model citizen to me."

"So as a reward, I end up bankrupt, with no workers, and hunted down by Russian Mafia."

"In the long run what choices do you have?"

"None. I can't go on doing business in that way and I've known that for a while. In the meantime it's Christmas and Santa's brought you to me."

"You haven't unwrapped me yet. I might be some Trojan horse."

"I love horses, they've made and lost me a couple of fortunes."

"So Max Muswell, let's start unwrapping Christmas there. Once upon a time there was a little cockney boy in the East End of London...."

He was still talking when they arrived at the house in Dulwich Village. He immediately put on a chef's apron and set about opening cans of coconut milk and preparing fish, prawns, garlic, ginger, and onions.

She watched his competence and speed with his chopping knife. Could he have been alone with only Justin for the past ten years? The pot was on the stove and he took off the apron. He took her hand and led her through to the hall.

"I just happened to see an old gipsy woman selling mistletoe. What a bit of luck, eh?"

She looked up into his eyes. The green plant hung from the lamp above them. She wanted him so much, maybe too much. This time the kiss was sensual, his thigh a little forward to let her press if she felt desire. She pressed as his hand came behind her to pull her in, to add that erotic hint to the wet touch of their lips and urgency of tongues in a tease of passion. She knew what was going on in her panties and ran her hand down to his waist, pressing her thumb closer to his cock, moving to the center to press the rock hard acknowledgement of her female power. He gave a deep dark growl as he kissed her neck and ran his hand up through her hair.

"You're risking getting that dinner a lot later."

"I'm in no hurry, Max."

He held her away a little. His face had softened but projected a lust for her. How she loved to say his name, like saying a name made her not alone, made her part of someone else. Emotionally she was in deep shit. Now he ran his hands down both her cheeks, stroking them as if she were some priceless thing that he couldn't quite believe.

"I want you so much, Paula. I saw you on that bus that night with those kids and how all those folk loved and respected you and now I want you physically, like I'm touching something too special."

"Max, I'm just a woman. It's lovely you feel that way. I want you too."

He pulled her back into his arms and held her tight.

"I'm better with men. With men I'm going to be top dog and nobody's going to even catch my eye. A woman like you is a different thing."

"I should bloody well hope so."

He brought his lips to hers again. With her eyes closed she was floating not above the earth but above life. She could feel the brute strength of his muscles. She could just melt into him and let him take her away. He went to the kitchen and turned off the stove. He took her hand and led her up the wide curved stair. The base of her belly pulsed with an excitement and absolute lust. He opened the door to a wonderfully furnished bedroom. He smiled with a slight nervousness.

"It's been a while," he said.

"Me too."

The curtains were open and a crescent moon shone through the bare branches of a large tree.

"Since the divorce, you know, I've not wanted to risk that loss again," he said.

"Let's put off the light and be together under the moon. Maybe you won't notice that my perfection is an illusion."

They undressed in the half light. She reached across the bed to stroke her hand down his back. He joined her under the duvet and brought his lips to hers as his hand soothed her breast and ran down across her belly. He teased a little at the frontier of her sex, kissing her deeply. She felt for his cock. The ruthless thickness jolted her, made her burn with her need to be filled. She shared the wet warmth of his tongue as his hand slid to her hot groove. He groaned at the luscious pleasure of her hot fluid flesh. His touch was gentle but firm, a stage whisper of passion. He was propped on his elbow watching her as he caressed and pressed her little shaft and bud. His cock strained and pulsed with the same rhythm. She touched him in the same quickening dance of need. She could see his strong male head and face in the quarter light of the room. He was sharing, courting, and following her unstoppable climb. Now she was closed to everything but her own body. The pressure was building and building, beyond anything she'd known in the past. He excited her higher than she'd known was possible. She could hear the sound of her wetness ticking up the steps to her release. She was so wet, he was so hard. His lips came to hers. She caressed his tongue with hers, she just held the brink for a delicious second and spilled out her sound against his lips as sobs of joy jerked her body in ripples of ecstasy. He hummed a deep note of pleasure as he soothed the helpless waves of subsiding lust back into her flesh. His hand had slowed but not stopped. She needed him inside but he was rolling her back up that soft mindless slope, pushing her as if his hand were on her back, guiding her on and on to that point where she would have to fall back. The point was near, she needed a final touch, a shred more of pressure. She began to masturbate his cock, urging him to know her mind. She was bringing him up that same slope, she was bringing herself off with a cock, she could smell their sex musk. She was beginning to come and come, yes bursting out of her soul in a howl of throbbing, sobbing release. She needed him inside her now. He responded to her signals and held his weight above her. His upright cock found her entrance and filled her, held her fixed and open. She pulled his buttocks, feeling the rock hard power of his muscle. He was moving inside her, making her submit, making her focus on that sweet spot inside. She was close and he was driving on harder.

"Paula, I'm going to come in you. Oh my lover, I'm going to let go in you, my lover, my lover."

She felt his shudder and heard his deep voice moaning out his ecstasy. She envisioned the pulse of his seed pouring into her hot belly as she spilled over into helpless waves of orgasm.

He sighed and dropped his lips between her breasts.

"Sweet wonderful woman, sweet wonderful woman. Stay with me."

She kissed his forehead. How nervous he seemed about her.

"You're one hell of a man, I must say."

"I didn't know if I'd be any use," he said with a broad smile.

"I'd say you were ten times anything I've ever known."

He lay back chuckling. Probably he thought it was flattery, but she was serious.

"You're kind to an old man. You turn me on so much."

"Hold that thought. I'll never complain."

"Really?"

"Why would I? You're gentle and strong all wrapped up in one. I've never had sensations like that."

"Never?"

"Never."

He drew her over to lay her head on his chest. Still the moon was behind the branches of the tree.

"Making love like that in the dark, is kind of like love, isn't it? Like you're feeling something you can't see or describe but you know exactly what it is," he said.

"You're the most unusual man I've ever met Max Muswell. You're fearless and tough but you're almost a bit of a poet."

"They gave me a list of possibilities when I was a kid and I could tick three boxes. No one asked me if I could read so I just went for it at random. That's a kind of a joke but so many people are limited by what's on the list they get handed."

"You're so right. Mine said bus driver and cop."

"I got three choices on my list."

"You're older than me. They cut it down to two to save money."

"You're funny. Let me cuddle up and rub you back. I meant it when I said stay with me."

"I meant it when I didn't say no but it depends what you mean. I'm not looking for any other relationship and I'm seeing where this goes, Max."

"I can't ask for more than that, can I?"

"You're making me happy, scarily happy."

"I know what you mean, Paula. Don't imagine I'm not afraid of losing this feeling."

"Better keep it somewhere safe then."

# CHAPTER 9

It had been so long since she'd woken up with a man. Her body felt serene but exulted. She could never have imagined that the male presence of him could arouse her and make her burn with desire and sheer animal lust to a point of exhaustion. He had loved her body with his lips and tongue, his cock had filled her. She'd driven him to heights of desire and release and shared his need and tenderness as they had slept wrapped together. She would never ever feel the same way, never ever see a film or read a story and say that real people never felt like that. She was a true lover now, a woman who had known the welding heat of fusion with a man. It wasn't a modern vision of a woman. She'd submitted, opened herself, abandoned herself to the hard spilling joy of him. She'd come so many times, driven on by his lust for her, his desire dragging him ruthlessly to fill her and kiss the essence from her convulsing soul. She could have lived her life without ever knowing what was sleeping inside her. Something told her that the road ahead wouldn't be smooth and could be disastrous. All the same she would view her future with the eyes of a completely awakened woman.

She was in the office by nine o'clock wearing jeans and a jumper. She ran a check on the minibus she'd followed. It was no surprise that it was registered to a cousin of the McCarthy clan. If this guy was the transport operation, it would be interesting to know his daily routine. Chief Superintendent Jack Miller presented himself at her side with a cup of tea.

"Suddenly everything is happening. Scotland Yard gobbled it all up and even better young Wayne McCarthy ended up in hospital last night."

Her heart stopped. Max had given one of them a bloody lip or so he'd said.

"What with?"

"Fractured jaw and cheekbone. Couldn't have happened to a nicer young man. Whoever did it must have some balls and some fast fists. There are three more brothers and a mob of cousins."

She shook her head.

"Has he said who did it and why?"

"No, of course not. There's no crime complaint but police got a call to the hospital 'cause the mob were causing trouble slapping nurses, fighting security staff, and demanding that Wayne went straight to the front of the queue."

"Lovely people, eh?"

"A couple got themselves locked up, but none of the main men. The good news is that we've got a surveillance team going to look at that bus. We don't want you running any more red lights and upsetting young master Crispin Bissel. What I need from you is a name of someone who uses the McCarthy agency, who might be prepared to help us. That might not be too easy, Paula."

"Leave it with me for a few hours, guv. I'll have a scout around and get back to you by lunchtime."

"Good girl. I'm sorry, I know that was sexist, elitist, and probably fucking fartist."

"I forgive you. Your true human self slips out if you're not concentrating on the PC."

"That's what I said, fartist. I'll catch you soon. Don't let your tea get cold."

He was quite a man. There were still too many people who knew his work rate and courage for anyone to try and get him out over a careless word. He'd probably made an enemy of Inspector Crispin Bissel, and the new squeaky clean teetotal vegan crew were dangerous. She called Max.

"We need to talk about Wayne McCarthy."

"It's not a nice subject."

"It wasn't a split lip"

"Yeah, I'm sure he cut his lip."

"He fractured his jaw and his cheekbone."

"He's a silly boy. He was a British light heavyweight champion boxer. He kept coming and I kept popping him. He must have swollen up a bit when he got home."

"Are you still willing to do the business against them?"

"I said I would and that's what I meant. I'm at my racing stables in Epsom. Why don't you run down and take my witness statement?"

"I guess I could. Have you heard from Justin?"

"Yeah, he's cool. Rachel's taking him to see the Manchester United football stadium today."

"OK, I'll come down and interview you formally. No extras you understand."

"Honey. All my forces are drained. I'm like Samson after Delilah cut all his hair off."

"Your hair is already cropped off."

"I was being poetic. What I meant was after she'd exhausted him with her irresistible passion."

"No more broken jaws."

"I'm too weak."

She'd only left him at her front door a couple of hours ago and now her heart soared at the thought of seeing him again. She told Jack Miller where she was going and added that Max was their man. The old detective smiled.

"I knew his dad. East End boy, hard as nails, heart of gold. Young Max was a bit of a tear-away and had a reputation as a fighter. Broke his heart when his mum died young. Those poor hard boys learned the code to worship a woman and fight like a man. I didn't know he owned Meadowchef. He's the sort of character who'd have broken Wayne McCarthy's jaw. He'd get a medal from me. You go for it, Paula. We've got the immigration guys coming up from Croydon about five o'clock. I'm pushing them to give those poor bastards a bit of slack even if it's only the right to stay for a year. If they get a bit of amnesty they might talk."

"We'll have to watch out for defense lawyers saying we've used that as a bribe, guv."

"Too true. If there's such a thing as ghosts I'm coming back as a phantom vigilante."

She had to agree. It was sad that a man who'd given all his life and soul to battling crime felt defeated by the system. Maybe the likes of Max Muswell offered a better alternative?

She pulled out of the yard and headed south toward the open country on the edge of London. Epsom was famous for the Derby horse race where thousands of Londoners rubbed shoulders with the royal family and celebrities of the world, on the open downs. On the first Saturday of June each year England gambled on the great race, as the Queen watched her own horses compete against the cream of thoroughbreds. Two years ago the winning horse had been owned and trained by a certain Max Muswell. Even after the night of love and abandoned passion she'd just passed with him, the thought of his charismatic fearlessness made her woman soul rise up and sing.

On the green hills outside of London the air was still crisp and frosty. The GPS on her cell guided her to the equestrian complex which to her eyes looked like a huge farmyard with stables on three sides. A guy was leading a beautiful tall and sleek horse from a stable, crows called from tall bare trees into an ice blue sky. This was a different world of calm and wealth. She saw the Rolls-Royce parked outside an old-fashioned farmhouse. The roof was thatched with straw like something out of a rural scenes wall calendar. She pulled up alongside a gross black Range Rover with alloy wheels, mirrored windows and flashy chrome fittings. She put her hand on the hood. It was still very warm. Her cop instincts told her there was something out of place. Hadn't Max talked about a vehicle like this following Justin from the park? This was a villain's vehicle. She took a photo on her cell and went to the door of the house and banged with a big iron knocker. No one came. She felt a sense of unease. The guy with the horse had mounted up and ridden out into the countryside. Still the crows were calling. Things were quiet, just too quiet. She skirted the building. At the rear were French windows looking out onto the serene beauty of Epsom Downs. Inside was a utility room opening out into a kitchen. She tried the door, her heart racing. It opened. She knew she should call for backup but there would be nothing close by. In any event what help was she asking for? She heard voices, several angry men with London accents. She had to think. Her guess was that the McCarthy boys had turned up to exact revenge for what Max had done to one of the brothers. If there had been no violence so far she had no reason to arrest them. The last thing she wanted was to expose the police interest in their employment agency before they were ready to pounce. She took her police warrant card from her pocket. She moved silently through the kitchen. The voices were in the next room. It was Max speaking.

"You ain't got the fucking balls. You know what your brother got and you'll get the same. I'll beat you all to a fucking pulp. If you get away I'll catch up with you and blow your brains out. Now which of you bits of shit wants to try me?"

Paula stepped into the room.

"Gentlemen, you should get your doorbell fixed. I had to let myself in."

Everyone in the room was standing facing Max. She saw Billy McCarthy whom she'd met briefly on the balcony of the flats in Peckham, and his brother Ross. There were two other guys she didn't know.

"What the fuck?" said one of them.

"Police. Metropolitan police, sir. I'm looking for Mr Muswell on quite an urgent matter. It's about a fraudulent trading account. We have a man in custody and the clock is ticking. I'm sorry to interrupt your meeting."

"Not guilty, officer. I ask you, gents, you can never get a copper when you need one and when you don't want one they're all over you."

The McCarthy crew stared at her dumbfounded. She kept her police ID open and let them gaze at it.

"Sorry boys. Looks like we're going to have to finish our business later," said Max.

He was standing by an old-style fireplace where there was a wood-burning stove. She noticed a shotgun leaning against the wall next to a baseball bat.

"Mr Muswell's going to have to come with me, guys. Looks like some idiot has cloned one of his business accounts. He shouldn't be too long."

She could see Billy McCarthy turning ideas over in his head. She estimated he wouldn't want any kind of war with the police.

"The sooner we get started the sooner you'll be able to get back to work, Mr Muswell."

"We'll be back later then," said Brother Ross.

"I'll get the kettle on, boys. Might even offer a nice bit of cake."

"Sorry, gents," she added.

One by one the sullen-faced men turned and walked to the door.

"I'll see you to your car and get a bit of air," said Max.

She watched him walk them to the Range Rover. She fired off a video on her cell. If they came back in ten minutes and murdered her, some useful evidence would be in the cloud. Max stood waving goodbye with an evil smug grin on his face, as the thugs pulled away. He put his hands in his pocket and strolled back to the house. He was so sexy in a wax jacket and blue jeans.

He took her in his arms.

"You're some sort of superwoman. You saved those poor bastards from some serious pain."

"Max, even you can't take on four men. I don't want to talk about the shotgun and the baseball bat."

"Someone got to scare the crows off the crops, and I like a bit of a ball game on a sunny day, Paula."

"Look, I simply never saw them, OK. We've got a surveillance team on the job. In a couple of days we'll be ready to go in and do a proper job on the McCarthy's operation."

"I didn't ask these jerks to show up here."

"I know that."

"You bloody saved me, didn't you?"

"Can't think why. You're a ... you're a bloody tough fearless guy, I do have to say that."

"Yeah, if you hadn't turned up, I'd have put up a fight but you and I both know what could have happened. This is my problem, Paula. I've got Justin. He'd have no one and the way he is he's never going to grow up, is he? We've only got each other. I'd die for him, but I can't die for him, if you see what I mean."

"You're a good man, Max, and I respect you for the good in you."

"And I'm a violent bastard and I know you don't respect that. I don't expect you to."

She shook her head. If only her feelings were that simple. In reality his brute fearlessness thrilled her although she hated to admit it to herself.

"Max, you're up against a mob of animals. I'm not going to make some righteous judgment of you."

He opened his arms to her.

"Come here, you lovely woman. God, you're giving me some lessons. You work with your head and cool courage. That stunt you pulled was fantastic."

She softened into his arms.

"How can you be such a rock hard man to those thugs and feel so, so loving to me."

"I'm a man, Paula. A man worships and protects his woman. That's the old code. The world out there is different matter."

"Should I be afraid of you? I'm asking you that question, but believe me I'm asking myself."

Had he really said *"his woman"*? Just how was he seeing her in his life?

"I don't ever want you to be afraid of anything. You can moan about my choice of socks or the lack of vegetables in my diet and I'll take it."

"Why should I be interested in all that?"

"Women get fads for that kind of thing if they stay around a man for long."

"Who says I'd ever be that interested in you?"

"Well, you've started by saving my life and keeping Justin with a father. You'd have to work up to the socks and the veg."

She softened herself into his arms.

"Oh, Max."

His powerful hand massaged her back and shoulders. Only now was she unwinding from the adrenalin that her fear had pumped into her blood.

"I'll drive you up to the police station. I don't want you here for your little tea party with the boys. I do need a statement and there's going to be a meeting with the immigration authorities and I'll get the boss to bring you in, if you don't mind. Please Max, keep within the law or everything will be over."

"Over between you and me?"

"Of course. I'm a cop. I'm a cop."

"I wouldn't want things to end between you and me."

His voice was slow, deep, and serious. She held his eyes and felt herself in a dance with him, following him.

"There's only one way to show me you're serious about that and that's by your actions or lack of them."

"Thank you, Paula."

"You're an odd guy. You don't need to thank me."

"A man always has to thank a woman. A woman chooses in the end."

# CHAPTER 10

His statement to police was an absolute game-changer. If they got him to give it as evidence, the McCarthy boys would be away for at least a decade. He sat with a coffee as she recorded his account of his relationship with them. Their agency was already supplying labor when he'd bought the business. He'd tried to throw them out, but at first they'd offered sweeteners.

"What sort of sweeteners?"

"Girls, they offered me a virgin, fifteen years old. She was a shivering little wretch."

"What happened to her?"

"God knows. I thought of grabbing her and sending her back home. They said she was Albanian. She had no papers and the local thugs out there would take it out on her family."

Then they'd tried threats, beaten up his ex-manager, torched one of the trucks. They sent SMS messages just setting out his home address and asking if Justin was OK. It was then he'd realized that he couldn't risk the lad, and accepted their terms. The statement ended with an account of their latest offer of compulsory extra staff.

"Maybe we won't mention Wayne McCarthy's injuries," she said.

"No, perhaps not. I was a bit disappointed he didn't go to hospital unconscious."

When the statement was finished she left him and took it to Detective Superintendent Jack Miller. He read it and almost lit up with glee.

"This is a work of art. This is the fucking fairy for the top of the tree. How the fuck did you get a man like Muswell to come across with this? Perhaps I don't want to know?"

"You don't want to know, guv."

"You're bloody something else you are, gal."

He reached down into the bottom drawer of his desk and pulled out a bottle of whisky. He poured two ultra-generous glasses.

"You deserve this, Paula. We've got a meeting at five o'clock. The surveillance team have been out all day and the immigration lads are coming in. There's some high flyers from Scotland Yard media relations and, do you want the bad news?"

"I'd love it."

"Inspector Crispin Bissel asked to be involved and to be honest, if I say no, he'll run crying to the district commander. I'll probably need a couple of his shift guys anyway when it comes to smashing doors in. Is there anyone I should want?"

"Basher and Vic-the-nick. They'd die for the job, guv. Is there any chance Max Muswell could be there? We need him and we'll be raiding his depot and leaving him without any staff."

"Yeah, why not? One of the Yard press guys is a civilian. Is there something between you two?"

"Nah, not really."

"Fuck off, Paula, there's something in your eye these last few days."

"You know how it is, guv."

"Good girl. Get stuck in 'cause ...'cause there's no slow motion replays in a cop's life."

She slugged back the whisky. It was nearly time for the conference. She collected Max and headed for the briefing room. He reached out and took her hand.

"This is a first for me. I can't believe I'm in a cop station on the right side of the bars."

"I'm not sure which side of the bars is best."

He stopped and pulled her to him for a kiss. She heard a step behind her. Why did it have to be Inspector Bissel? Max thrust out his hand to shake.

"Fuck me, boss, I could have sworn I saw a bit of mistletoe up there. Must have fallen down. Didn't fall in your shirt pocket did it?

Max gripped the Inspector's hand. He winced and recoiled.

"Sir, this is Max Muswell. He's helping police in this enquiry."

Inspector Bissel gulped wordlessly. Max was still crushing his hand.

"Is this man going to be at the briefing?"

"He is," said Max.

Paula couldn't help but laugh at the contrast between the two men. Maybe it was education or maybe it was pure testosterone. Either way there was no contest. Max let him go and they filed into the room. Jack Miller opened the meeting.

"Ladies and gents. We all know we're talking about the McCarthy boys. We're going to smash these bastards once and for all. Just let me welcome our friends from Scotland Yard and a special thanks and welcome to Mr. Max Muswell. He's a prominent business man and is vital to our operation. Stand up, Max, so the boys and girls can see you."

Max stood up. There was a general murmur and a few claps. She heard Basher's voice.

"Respect man."

"Yeah, respect to you, Max," said Vic-the-nick.

She hadn't realized that these men held him in esteem.

"You keeping that left hand up, Bash?" said Max.

This was his own territory. The boys knew him and his reputation as a fighter. This blood and sweat boys' world was where he was a top dog. She glanced at Inspector Bissel. His face was white and strained as he recorded something in his official notebook. It was wrong but it thrilled her to be Max's lover, the woman at the gentle end of a respected hard man.

"Right, that's your moment of fame, Max. Let's start with the surveillance team."

A keen-looking sergeant detailed what they had uncovered.

"These idiots are so blatant they just march these poor souls about. We've identified four addresses and about sixty workers. We've also identified two brothels where this clan supplies young girls. We've a list of half a dozen places who use the slave labor. To be honest, gents, we're looking at thugs who are so confident that no one's going to bother them, that they run it like it was a completely normal business. We've linked their supply to a couple of Russian gangsters and an Albanian pimp. The question is how deep do we cut and what resources can we call on?"

Jack Miller was on his feet again.

"That's a question for the bosses at Scotland Yard. Let's keep in mind, ladies and gentlemen, that we're talking about poor hungry people at Christmas time. It is within our power to bring some happiness and justice to people who have no way of helping themselves. Does anyone in this room not share these ideals?"

There was a murmur of agreement. Paula watched the media guys in some kind of frenzy on their tablet computers.

"Let's hear from the immigration guys. Can you help us?"

A stout middle-aged bald man walked to the front of the room. He had a weariness that everyone who'd toiled hopelessly at the coal face understood.

"This world is a pretty horrible place if you're poor. The poor have got it good. The people we're talking about here, had *nothing* until they grabbed a desperate chance to get just a little crumb of something. Poor bastards shipped in containers or lured to the big cities of the world with an offer of work. We are only too aware of the endless revolving door of exploitation and deportation. Here's the bottom line. You guys want to bust some crooks who get rich on these pawns. No one will talk if they're going to be deported back to nothing. Our recommendation is that we offer temporary permission to remain to these individuals. We are applying to the government for clearance. The decision is political and way above my head."

Jack stood up.

"When will you know?"

"Get your top cops in there with your feel-good media-show angle. You know the truth. You bust a celebrity singer for touching a girl forty years ago. You go in with the cameras alongside the cops. Police work is a reality show. If the politicos think it's good PR we'll get the nod in a couple of days and the ministers will be powdered-up to play Santa for the cameras."

"I thought I was a bloody cynic," Max whispered.

"Is he wrong?"

"Nah, he's spot on, gal. Dear God, my Christmas prayer, please let me drive my fist into Billy McCarthy's face and burst his nose."

Jack Miller was wrapping up the meeting.

"We know the addresses, we know the villains, we need the politics. I'm sure our colleagues from the Public Relations department will have noted our determination to operate in the seasonal spirit. As soon as we have a green, or a red light, I'll call you all back. Thanks and have a nice evening."

The room emptied out. Max shook hands and more or less held court with some of the guys. She'd had no idea of his status in this man's world of reputation and respect.

"I wouldn't be helping out you load of losers if you hadn't sent me a sexy undercover woman to soften me up," he declared.

The fan club laughed, slapped backs, high-fived, touched fists, shadow boxed.

She watched Inspector Crispin Bissel slink way. He was not a happy bunny. At last Max turned to her.

"Nearest pub, nearest pizza joint, and your place for bed."

"Last offer I had like that was a sack of brussel sprouts so I guess you've topped that."

He threw his arm around her shoulder. God, she felt possessed and wanted. This man made her soul lift off.

"No pub. Italiano, candlelight with a shared bottle of Chianti."

"Christ you're a precious creature. I know a place. Watch out 'cause candlelight makes a girl irresistible and men fall in love."

"And then fall out of love in the daylight."

"You make this life what you want it to be. Right now there's never going to be another dawn."

# CHAPTER 11

They ate at the Caravaggio in Camberwell, Church Street. The last thing she wanted to talk about was the police or the mission ahead of them. She hadn't realized her hunger as they both set about a traditional spaghetti.

"You know I feel like we're those two dogs in Lady and the Tramp," he said.

She laughed.

"Max, I'd have never put you down as a Walt Disney fan."

"Hey, who isn't when they've got kids? Justin loves that movie."

"He's a lovely young man."

"Yeah, he is. It's just been me and him for ten years."

His expression was soft without even a trace of the persona he showed to the world. Even so she hesitated to poke into what might be still a wound. While she was thinking he spoke again, holding her with his deep eyes.

"I'm guessing you don't want to ask me too much about him and my past with his mother. Don't ever be afraid of me, Paula."

"Look, I'm curious about you. Everyone needs to come out in their own time and that may be never. Whatever your feelings or actions around Justin, I would respect them."

He took a deep breath and seemed to make a final decision to talk.

"She wasn't perfect as a woman you know. I always knew that. She'd made herself something by using her charms and I'd pulled myself up with my fists. To be honest neither of us were the people we wanted to be, but we had ambition and determination. I respected and loved her for that. She'd been a porn star, but it's no worse than punching a guy just because you get paid to do it."

"I'd go along with that."

"Her agent got her this film role and she became Azzura Vermillion. She chose the name 'cause she liked them from paint pots at school. I've always remembered that because it helps to see that everyone you meet was a naive, hopeful kid once, whatever they've become. She met this film director Romano Poxato. He was an international jet-setter dude who knew everyone and it simply overwhelmed her. She wasn't a sophisticated girl."

"How did you feel about that?"

"Sad for me and sad for her. He dumped her and walked away. I've never wanted to prove that Justin wasn't my son. He'll always be the son of my wife. What pride could I have in myself just to walk away from him?"

"I shouldn't say it but it's a bit of a Christmas story, isn't it? I used to wonder what Joseph made of Mary."

"I'd never seen it that way. I don't do religion, but yeah, Justin's a gift out of the universe. You can see all men and woman as brothers and sisters if you want to think that way."

"Wow, is that how you see it?"

"Justin will never grow up. He's an innocent and that would be the way he'd see it. In a fight you batter each other and then at the end you have respect. You both wanted to win but that man is your brother whether you've won or lost."

What a complex man he was, yet his complexity was rooted in his simplicity. He had warrior codes of honor and he didn't try to cover himself in clever theories.

"Max, I respect you so much for the way you care for Justin."

"Thank you. It means a lot for someone like you to say that."

"Someone like me? There's not a lot of difference between you and me, believe me."

"Justin's mine. You care about everyone. You care about the kids you drive on the community bus, you care about the people exploited by the McCarthys."

"Well, I don't have a special person to care about, do I?"

The words had just jumped out of her. In that moment she'd said it all about her life and she hadn't meant to express that depth of herself. Until that moment she'd never tried to describe her feelings in words to anyone. She was already in deep emotional danger with this man. Now he could counterpunch and her guard was down. He didn't answer at once, but reached across and took her hand.

"If you don't want anyone in your life, I can understand that. You've had disappointments yourself. You can choose your path, but I'm here at the crossroads."

He was right about one thing. She was at a crossroads and he was sure standing there.

"I might go left, right, or straight on."

"A chivalrous gentleman always walks on the outside of a lady. I can take either hand so I've got it covered."

"You are beautifully old-fashioned and politically incorrect, Max."

"And I'm never going to change."

His eyes were steady and kind. She could hold his gaze forever and not move from this moment.

"I'd never want you to change. We've got a tough few days ahead. I'm trying to keep everything in different compartments of my life until this job is over."

"Let's see where we are by Christmas, eh?"

She nodded agreement. It was a short walk to her little home and they didn't have a car.

"Are you happy to slum it in my little burrow?"

"I'd love your little burrow."


They walked hand in hand along the Camberwell Road. Their relationship seemed completely natural. The idea of having him beside her for the night thrilled and aroused her. He was used to luxury and her little bed sit was pretty much mean street. Even so, he wanted to know her and this was how she was and how she lived. Once inside he held her and kissed her with his surprising gentleness. He found and took her lips rather than pressing. There was a tentative shyness about him that always made her feel blatant and wanton in her own lust for him. She watched him walk to the window and look down into the street.

"This is great, being up here in this little perch, watching all the traffic like blood pulsing along an artery."

She moved behind him, pressing him into her, running her hands down his waist and sides of his hard muscular thighs. She crept back up to his groin, couldn't resist teasing over his hard cock, bursting for freedom from his clothing.

"You're a naughty girl, you know. I might have to deal with you harshly."

"I'd better get myself ready then."

She slipped away to the shower. There was no way she was going to reveal herself to him unprepared. Her wetness and arousal quite shocked her. Even as a newly married young woman she'd never had this response. She'd never known such a response was possible. How could you know that a partner wasn't fully turning you on, if you hadn't had other partners? She had to be careful how she touched herself. She was so far along the road that she could get to a point where she couldn't stop. She'd soon realized in her marriage, that she was turning herself on with fantasy and self-release more than she was with her husband. It was a behavior that she'd maintained as a guilty secret. In bed with him she'd been already defused and she knew her response to him had been tepid. How many women lived such a life and had never found a man like Max? Could a woman ever let go of such joy and passion, let alone boil the pot over by adding emotional love?

She wrapped herself in a robe and presented herself to him. He was seated on the bed holding out his arms in invitation. He pulled her groin to his lips and opened her gown.

"Oh God, oh God, Max."

She was already so close. The wet heat of his tongue found her clit, kissed her lips, traced circles, ran the length of her groove to her entrance and back, now homed in on her rhythmic need for certainty, for understanding of her tension, knowing she was holding the door shut, letting the pressure mount until she pushed out a cry.

"Fuck yeah, you're making me come."

The orgasm trembled down her thighs and up into her chest. She brought her own hands to her nipples as the thrill zinged between her breasts and her sex. Still he was there, his lips and tongue caressing and fondling her flesh and her flowing juice. She brought her hands to his head to hold the sweet joy of him. He was groaning deep loving worshipping sounds. His hands had come up to her nipples, mimicking the same pulse as his tongue on her love button and aching little shaft. The tease was so delicious. She could just let it go but she wanted it to climb to the peak before she let it....

"Oh, oh. Oh God, I'm coming in my pussy, Max. Oh, don't stop."

She bent double over him, her breasts pressing into his flesh. She ran her nails down the length of his back as spasms of pleasure tore the strength from her legs. The feel of his hard body under her fingers thrilled her as she abandoned all restraint. She longed for him to fill her. She was open, needing the ruthless heat of his cock. He moved aside and let her spread herself on the bed. His lips came to hers. The juice was her own and she loved to know it on his skin, where he had tasted the essence of her. She felt for his cock. Her flowing sex had called to him and he was wet with urgent desire for release inside her. He had pulled off his clothes and held his weight above her. His cock was long, thick, and rigid. His angle naturally found her and slid in with a filling sense of wholeness. He pulled out and in, teasing and satisfying her need. She couldn't hold back her desire to come. She reached for her clitoris to press against his shaft, her motion transforming into an urgent masturbation as she let go in her belly and with her bud.

He pulled away and rolled her on her side, spooning into her back, his rock hard penis seeking her once more. She raised her leg as his hand came around to caress her with the same drive as his cock. Once again as he hit her G spot, his hand raised her hard clit to a shriek of release. Her helpless flood of ecstasy drove him on to his own climax. He was breathing harder onto her neck, his hand massaging her shoulder. His lips and teeth were against her flesh as he tightened, tightened, and drove in to his limit.

"Lover woman, Paula, I'm coming."

She felt the springing of his seed in her belly and shook with her own spasm of orgasm.

"Do it, Max. Fuck, do it in me."

For a while his hard cock still twitched with tremors of abandoned pleasure inside her. This was the greatest sense of calm she'd ever known. The fullness had spread to her soul and merged into a drifting blur of sleep and oblivion. His breath was against her back, his lips kissing, his tongue tasting her body, his hand cupping her breast. There need never be anything further in this world. She'd been opened and filled. A yawning diffused ache in her had been found and soothed.

Slowly the world was returning. The light was now off but the blinds open. By chance this was the way they had been together before. She loved the sense of hanging between two worlds as if their joy of each other couldn't exist in the plainness of conscious life. He was stirring a little, but still held her tight and safe. He was murmuring as if to himself.

"Never leave me, please Paula."

She shifted and turned to face him. She knew what he'd said in his semi-conscious state.

"What, did you say something Max?"

He turned away and she spooned into him, stroking the fur of his hair.

"I think I said something. You're too wonderful for me, you know."

Then there was profound wonderful sleep. Who could leave a man who made a woman feel this way?

# CHAPTER 12

It was 4:00 a.m. when his cellphone began to ring. She could hear an excited voice of a male caller.

"Yeah, thanks, Joe. I'll be there," said Max.

"What is it?"

"That was my neighbor. Some kind soul has set fire to my Bentley. The fire brigade is still there. I just can't think who would want to do such a thing, can you?"

"Well, we know who, don't we? It's not going to be easy to prove, but you never know."

"There's CCTV all around the house and outside."

"It goes without saying that the police will do their best."

She knew without asking, that Max would not be leaving the matter simply in the hands of the police.

They dressed quickly and took a cab from the taxi office across the street. A fire truck was still outside the house. Max told the cab driver to wait.

"What's the score?" he asked the chief.

"Accelerant fire, looks like they smashed their way in and chucked in a gallon of gas."

"Definitely not accidental?" asked Paula.

"No chance."

The beautiful vehicle was completely destroyed. A local police unit turned up.

"Mr Muswell, it may be this was deliberate. Were you at home?" asked a young male/female constable.

"No."

"I'll need a statement. If this was arson, do you have any idea who could be responsible?"

Max shook his head.

"Kids, I expect. No point in you wasting your time, officer."

His manner was still and cold. He wasn't shouting or making threats. Now she saw him as the fighter, the ruthless dispassionate avenger. His skin was pale, his body containing an awful violence primed to explode.

"Max, we need to explain a few things to him."

"You can deal with that. The CCTV controls are in the back office. I've got an important early meeting."

"Max, we need to think about how we're going to deal with this."

"I've told you. Give the officer a cup of tea and check out the CCTV. I'm a business man and I have a meeting. It's that simple. End of discussion."

"Max...."

"Officer, Paula's one of your own. I have to get away for a breakfast conference. She'll take it from here."

He took her forearm and held it as he looked her in the eye and handed her his house keys.

"Business. My business," he said.

He turned and walked to the taxi. A few seconds later he was out of sight. The fire crew stored their hoses and left the scene.

"Hi, I'm Paula Middleton, PC 866L. I'm stationed at Brixton."

"I'm Charlotte Morley from Southwark. As you can see, I'm PC 581M"

"Come on in, Charlotte. I hope you're ready for a long story."

She'd made a decision. Some small part of her wanted to hold back her fear that Max would exact direct revenge on the McCarthy clan. As a cop talking with a fellow officer she had to maintain professional integrity. If he broke the law then she would have to be against him. She fumbled with the unfamiliar keys and locks. An ear-splitting siren began to screech. Why the hell had he just gone off and left her? She found the alarm de-activator and headed for the kitchen.

"First thing is a big fix of coffee."

"You're a star," replied PC Morley.

Paula guessed her age at about twenty-five. The first thing she needed to explain was why she was there with Max.

"Mr Muswell is helping police with an investigation into a gang of crooks called the McCarthys."

"I'm always seeing their name on intelligence briefings. Didn't one of them get beaten up?"

"You know about that?"

"Yeah, some older cops cheered when the sergeant read out the report."

"Charlotte, the McCarthys may believe that it was Max who did it. I'm not saying he did do it, but that may be why they've torched the car."

"Right, I understand, I think."

"Look, I can't mess you around, OK? Max and I are in a relationship but we've only just got together. I've no evidence that he did it. We're setting up an operation to bust the whole clan for trafficking, prostitution, and maybe other stuff will come out of the woodwork."

"Mr. Muswell has a meeting this morning?"

"Yes, he had to get away."

She kept her answer short. The young cop in front of her was more than capable of adding up the likely nature of the meeting. Inwardly she boiled with anger at his maverick departure. The whole show could crash if he got himself into trouble. And she would have to abandon him to his fate or even lock him up herself. She was a cop and if he didn't respect that, there could never be anything worthwhile.

She fixed the coffee and went through to an office to view the CCTV. The picture quality was good. At 02:45 hours a familiar old Ford Transit minibus pulls up opposite the house. Two men wearing stocking masks get out. One is carrying a gas can and the other has a baseball bat. They come to the Bentley on the front drive. One guy smashes the rear window with the bat. The other pours in the contents of the can. The first figure flicks a cigarette lighter and a ball of flame engulfs the scene.

"Bloody hell!" exclaimed the young officer.

They watched as the clothing and stocking mask of the second man burns. The first figure tears off his own mask and pushes his comrade to the ground and beats at his clothing. When the fire is out, they stagger away to the bus and scream away. The Bentley becomes an inferno.

"Pretty clear. They're complete morons. Why didn't he realize the vapor would ignite?" said Paula.

"That guy must be badly burned."

"Yes, he's one of the cousins. The guy with the bat is Ross McCarthy."

Now she needed to think. Did she call Max and assure him the police had all the evidence they'd ever need? Would the clear identification of the offender merely spur him on to take the matter into his own hands? She took out her cellphone and called him. It was no surprise that he didn't pick up. The young officer was talking on her police radio. She signed off and raised her thumb.

"We've got a unit at King's College Hospital. A guy's been dumped out of a Ford Transit. He's got serious burns and might not make it."

"Not too much doubt it's one of our suspects. We need to get that bus for forensic and pull in Ross McCarthy. I'll get to Brixton later to write you a statement and speak to Chief Superintendent Miller. I know the license plate on that Transit. Can I use you radio?"

She took the mic.

"Mike Delta this is Lima-eight-eight-six. Can you patch me through to MP for an all cars?"

"Go for it."

"All cars, all cars, urgent. Stop and detain Ford Transit minibus RC50LKN. Last seen King's College Hospital. Driver may be white male Ross McCarthy born 21st May, 1989, wanted for arson and criminal damage. Seal vehicle for crime scene investigation."

Once more she called Max's number, but he didn't pick up. Whatever happened at the end of this affair, he was going to get an ear-bashing. For now she had done what she could in terms of immediate police response. The next job was to get more coffee and print evidential copies of the CCTV footage. And wait for that bastard Max Muswell to turn up, get locked up or bite off more than he could chew and end up in the hospital, or the morgue. His life would be where it always had been and always would be—in his own pig stubborn hands.

Constable Charlotte Morley dropped her back at her flat. She looked at the tangled crumpled bed where she'd slept with him just a few hours ago. She could smell and sense his body. She slumped down where he had lain holding her. Why had she gotten involved with such a man? She'd achieved very little in life by many standards but now she could end up at zero. Somehow fate had dumped them together in the same sack. If she hadn't agreed to drive the bus to see the Christmas lights, if she hadn't agreed to go Brighton beach, if she hadn't had fabulous sex with him. She'd never even been a sexy woman until the bastard had come along. She'd had more orgasms with him than she'd had in a whole marriage. She was more sexed up as a female now than she'd been as a teenager. She could really loathe a man who'd done that to her.

# CHAPTER 13

She was at her desk at 7:30 a.m. to begin her statement. The world seemed bland and normal. A night-shift detective was filing a rape investigation, a coroner's officer was making calls trying to identify a homeless junkie found dead of cold and pneumonia. The normal background sound and elevator music of police life calmed her. Rapes, corpses, and robberies were her comfort zone. In the grand scheme of things, Max was nothing. When she finished her work, she went to the canteen for coffee and toast. A loud cheerful sergeant they all called Nunky was telling a tale to a laughing audience.

"Straight up, no word of a lie. He's got an earth-mover digger from a site up the road. He's gone down there and tipped the Range Rover on its roof and then smashed it to total fucking bits with the shovel. Then, while Billy McCarthy's still in bed, he's driven the digger right up to the front door and smashed his way into the house. The whole front fell in. Fucking McCarthy's only in there with some foreign girl who looked about twelve. Just for good measure he flattened some posh fountain in the front garden. The geezer gets out and calls to Billy while he's in bed in the rubble, saying if he wants some more it can be arranged. Then he gets back into the digger, drives it up the road, gives the foreman five hundred quid as a hire fee and to cover any scratches. Then cool as a vigilante cucumber, he wanders off to hail a cab."

"Pity he didn't put the shovel on Billy's head," said one officer.

"Does your heart good to see someone stand up for once," said another.

"Who did it then?" she asked.

"Hello, Paula. Don't usually see you on green shift. Did you fancy seeing some real men for a change?"

"Sounds like I came at the right time."

"Who wants to discover who did it boys and girls? Is there any traitor the room who wants to lock up the suspect?" said Nunky.

There were a few boos. The attitude of the crowd seemed clear.

"I'll bring you over a coffee, Paula. I'll fill you in."

"In your dreams, sarge. She's right above your league," came a voice.

Nunky winked and went for the coffees while she found a table. She knew more or less what she was going to hear.

"Paula, I might be talking out of place but a little birdie did tell me you might know a bloke called Max Muswell?"

"Yeah, I do."

"Like you had a bit of a clinch with him and that prick Inspector Crispin Bissel has run to the commander wanting you busted. I only know 'cause the secretary overheard him. From what I gather the commander told him to fuck off and jerk his dick if he was getting over-excited and didn't know how to deal with himself. Now, I may be wrong, and this is just between you and me."

She knew damn well that if Nunky knew it, everyone knew it.

"So who did Billy's house and car over?"

"Well, Max of course. He didn't wear any kind of disguise. The site foreman claims he didn't know him but if Max asks a man to keep his mouth shut, that's the end of the debate."

"Because he scares them or what?"

"You know how it is. I know we're all unisex these days but there's still a tough man's world out there. It's about respect. He's a fair man but harder than the sidewalk if you cross him. He knows what honor is and he expects a man to know it."

"Fucking hell, Nunky. So there's no witness statements?"

"Nah, and no complaint from the unfortunate victim. He told us he would deal with the matter privately. We scooped up the little girl and she's been put in care as a minor. Billy says she's a maid and must have lost all her clothes when the house collapsed. Poor little thing was only half formed if you know what I mean. The detectives will get interpreters and see what they can put together."

She decided to keep her own half of the story to herself. Even though Max was some sort of hero among the Desperate Dan-type cops, he was a dangerous outlaw. Any further relationship with him would end her career for sure. She began to see how legends of Robin Hood and Ned Kelly had become folklore. In the meantime there was the matter of the wider operation to release the slaves. Max was a critical element in that project. It was time to forget all about her personal life and get back to work. For a final time she called his number.

"Paula, you OK?"

"I'm OK, except I've been stupid to get involved with you. Everyone knows what you've done."

"Yeah, that's great isn't it? I love it when people understand me."

"You're a nut job. People don't do this sort of stuff."

"Can't have happened then. If it didn't happen, what are you fretting about?"

"Max, I'm a cop. I know a lot of the guys love you and all that but none of this is my style. We'll cooperate on our work, but it's over between me and you. No hard feelings and thanks for ... well thanks for the fantastic lovely stuff. You're a wonderful man in many ways."

"Thank you. That's fair if that's what you want. I respect a woman, and a woman chooses. I won't wrap you up in a load of fancy words, but you mean a lot to me, Paula. I've done my business like a man with some idiots who disrespected me. I'll never show you anger and I want you to walk away from me with good feelings in your heart."

Suddenly tears filled her eyes.

"Oh, Max, it just has to be this way, OK."

She couldn't say more and clicked off. In an ideal world she would never see him again. She took a deep breath and set off for the office. Inspector Crispin Bissel was sitting in her chair. She didn't need this.

"Constable Middleton, I must advise you that you are formally under investigation for gross professional misconduct in public office. It is alleged that you brought about the withdrawal of a complaint against you, by entering into an improper sexual relationship with the complainant. I have seen some of the evidence with my own eyes."

"You can fuck off. Is the district commander backing you on this?"

"The matter is being dealt with directly from Scotland Yard. I will not tolerate the way you and many officers here operate. This is not the wild-west saloon. The police operate under media scrutiny and there is no forgiveness of incorrect procedure. The new police controllers and managers will be untainted by old practices. I hereby notify you, that you are forthwith suspended from duty. You will not contact any police officer, come to the station or involve yourself with any police activity, professional or social."

"Well, I have to admit you've got some balls at least. You've got your beliefs and you're prepared to be hated and despised by most of your colleagues to pursue your own ambitions. Believe it or not I respect you for that. On the other hand you may be too green to have thought it through and I'll leave you to ponder that."

"I can't believe the attitude of you people here. It's like you're in the last century. The future is correctness, morality, and purity of conduct."

"Fuck all that shit. Jack Miller's going after the McCarthy boys for big, big, trafficking offences. He was going to put your face on TV. Just think of the career boost, guv. You might have fucked yourself up the ass but that's not my concern. You'd better talk to Jack Miller. In the meantime I can go and drive a community bus for some disadvantaged kids while you count your purity points."

She turned and began to walk away.

"Constable there are papers to serve and forms for you to sign."

"Stick them up your ass. If you want to stop me, get your cuffs out and prepare a cell 'cause you'll be in a fight. Look up my address and tell me the result of your investigation when you get the chance. Happy Christmas."

She walked on. She'd been horrible to him and she wasn't proud because he was a sad little kid who needed help. He'd been looking to bust an experienced cop to proclaim his new-broom philosophy. She was a mug for giving him the ammunition to fire. Many of the tough cops would have decked him and maybe he'd gone for her as a soft target. All the same she'd left herself open. The new world of perfect moral righteousness was a cruel, unforgiving place for a human.

She threw in her police ID at the desk sergeant. He looked up in astonishment.

"Paula—what the fuck?"

"I'm out of here until I hear different. See you."

She walked to the bus stop. She watched the big red 45 service new-style Routemaster pull in. She still had a skill and a way to get a living. She still had her friends: Irene from the bus and Sally the social worker. She still had the kids and the elderly from her community work. An hour ago an officer was trying to find any family for a young junkie who'd died alone. A friendless adolescent girl from Billy McCarthy's house had been put into a children's home. She knew that Irene would look up to Jesus and thank him, not for what she'd lost but for what she still had. She had a home at Christmas and many did not. She had enough money and many did not. She had no one special to share her life and she had no child. She needed a drink. She needed not to have one.

# CHAPTER 14

She called Irene.

"Tell the office I'm free until the end of term. It'll be great to be with the kids right up to Christmas."

"Sweet Jesus knew already. Poor old Ronald got sick today and I prayed. I got down and prayed just this minute. I'm going to get some twinkling lights for the bus and we're making Christmas happen for these sweet people, Paula."

She knew Irene had very little money.

"Leave the lights to me. I've got some somewhere and I'll dig them out. I'll see you in the morning."

She'd lied but it was a purpose in her life to find some stuff to decorate the bus. The modern traffic regulations forbade it but she wanted to go large. Let them drag her away in chains. Oh Max, fearless proud Max—he would understand.

She called Sally. More than anything she wanted someone on her side, even if she had done wrong in the eyes of the system.

"If you need a driver, call me and I'll try and help."

"That's a silly question 'cause I always need helpers. How about collecting some senior citizens from around Bermondsey for a Christmas dinner like in an hour's time?"

"Sure."

"Are you OK, Paula?"

"I'm OK. Well, actually I'm not. I'm suspended from duty. I'm not allowed to have any contact with anyone, so I kind of feel a bit lonely if I'm honest."

"Honey, you poor thing. What did you do for God's sake?"

"Long story. A guy complained about me. By chance I met him and we sort of got together. He dropped the complaint and the charge is, I sweetened him up by having a relationship with him."

"Is that illegal? What does he say about it?"

"I don't think they've asked him yet. These investigations take a long time and we've split up now anyway."

"Right, I'll be round after work unless you've got other plans."

"I'd love that. I really don't want to be on my own this evening. Am I pathetic?"

"You're a wonderful human being, Paula. I can't believe the police would do this to you."

"It's a system. No one cares who gets pushed under the train."

"Do you actually want to remain a cop? I think I'd be wondering if it was all worth it."

"What else have I got? A lot of those guys at Brixton are more or less my family. A lot of the folks I work with on the streets are friends. I just don't know. I've just got to man up and take it on the chin. I'm so sorry to be whining."

"We'll talk it all out tonight."

"Can you text me the addresses for your old folks. I'd better get going."

It was good to have a task to complete. Once she was rolling the bus through the streets of London, her mood lifted. She'd brought her CDs of Christmas hits and carols. She liked driving seniors because they always joined in to sing. Her route took her up across Blackfriars Bridge where they sang *"Away in a Manger."* As she pulled up in Clerkenwell, Brenda Lee was belting out *"Rocking Around the Christmas Tree."* The company and the music completely lifted her mood. Once the passengers were clear she found a supermarket and bought some battery Christmas lights to decorate the kids' bus. She added a dozen chocolate Santas to hand out on the last day. What a joyous freedom it was to be thinking about other people. The last thing she wanted was to reflect on her own situation. Despite everything that had happened, that bloody man kept intruding into her space. The touch of him, the sheer joy of being around him. His wild independence. His danger. Contacting him could only make things worse and open her to more allegations. Dear Lord, what a difference a few days could make in a lifetime. She knew he wouldn't give any evidence against her. She was sure he would just tell them to go away.

She'd been suspended, but in her heart she didn't believe they could make anything serious stick. Inspector Bissel had seen her kiss Max outside the meeting and she could get an official reprimand, or maybe be fined a day's pay for unprofessional conduct. It would be a small feather in his cap and that might be enough for him. It hurt her not to be involved in busting the McCarthy clan. It was only a week until Christmas and she wanted those people free and fed on Christmas Day. She knew it was no more than sentimental self-indulgence. Chief Superintendent Jack Miller would drive the job through and her presence would make no difference.

She drove back to Clerkenwell and picked up the old folk. A smiling old man presented her with a bouquet of flowers that somehow they had organized for her. Suddenly she broke down in tears and had to take a deep breath before she could set off.

"Thank you so much," she said.

"Thank you, my dear. I hope those are happy tears."

"Yes, yes of course. It's so nice to be wanted."

"Who wouldn't want a lovely girl like you?" he replied with a wink.

She laughed. He must have been well on the way to ninety.


It was mid-afternoon when she got home. She busied herself with the flowers and then poured herself a large vodka. This wasn't a pattern she wanted to establish in her life. The doorbell rang. Did she want company? She looked out of the window to the street. It was Jack Miller. She went to the door.

"Guv. I'm not supposed to see anyone."

"Fuck all that stuff. Can we talk for a couple of minutes?"

"Come in. It's good to see you."

He took a chair and pulled out a half-bottle of whisky from a poacher pocket inside his overcoat. He waved it at her.

"I've got a vodka thanks."

"Well, give me a glass. It's right uncouth to swig out of the bottle."

She laughed. For sure he had a problem, but she'd never seen him drunk.

"I hope you don't get busted for coming here."

"No chance. Look, we're going in on the McCarthy boys the day before Christmas Eve and you're going to be with us. Keep your head down and leave all this investigation shit to me. I'll tell you, Paula, there's people in tears back there over what's happened to you. I've promised everyone you'll be back and I make the same promise to you."

"I don't want anyone to get into trouble for me, guv. Crispin Bissel's still going to be there, isn't he?"

"We'll see about that. Much more important than him is you. I was having a chat with Max earlier. He knows what's happened and I've had to convince him not to deal with anything himself."

"We need Max to stay on our side and give evidence."

"We sure do and what he needs is to see you."

"He's too dangerous. You know what happened with the digger."

Jack Miller let out a bellow of laughter.

"What a classic. What a fucking classic! I'll tell you, Paula, it warmed my heart to see that place knocked down."

"I'm guessing that's not an official police statement."

"Not quite. Look, you're a grown woman and you don't need my advice. If you want to be with him just bloody well do it. He's spoken to me man-to-man and he wants to talk things through with you. I'll say no more."

"Thanks, guv."

"We're up to about eighty people now in four or five locations. On the day, we're going to need you on the females. At the latest you'll be back on duty the day before we go in. It will be the usual 4:00 a.m. style raid and to make it worse, we've got media film crews on each team and a couple of high profile reporters. They want to hit the breakfast shows with the first feel good footage. Policing is getting to be a part of bloody showbiz, with grandstand cops. I hate it, but we are where we are."

"If it gets those people free I can live with it."

He stood up, took a deep breath and went to the door.

"Four days and we pounce. If you want him, give the guy a break, Paula. Please, in the spirit of Christmas."

When he'd gone she slumped down on the bed. How could he be so sure she'd be back? Had he come mainly to deliver a message from Max? Of course she wanted him. If Justin was still away in Manchester, he would be alone like her. She stared at her cellphone. He always told her that a woman chooses. Sure, she had a choice to make.

# CHAPTER 15

She spent the evening with Sally and then did the early bus run with Irene. Once the kids were delivered to the community center, they set about decorating the interior. The day was dark with a cold wind. Even at midday, cars had headlamps on. When they switched on the strings of lights the effect was almost magical.

"It's going to blow those kids away when they get back on," said Irene.

"It'll be cool to see their faces."

Irene reached out and took Paula's hand.

"I prayed and sweet Jesus got you here today."

"Maybe it wasn't Jesus. Maybe it was me getting myself into trouble and getting suspended from work."

"Dear Lord, we can't see the plans he has for us. That little babe born in that stable went through suffering to bring love to this world. You do your best, you always choose the way of love with your good heart and you don't need to bother with questions."

"I wish I had your faith."

"You've got more than enough love in your heart. Jesus can see right through to that and you can't keep those eyes of his out with no words. Do you believe in love?"

"Yeah, I do."

"Epistle of John 4:7: *Everyone who loves has been born of God and knows God.*"

"I'll hold that thought, Irene."

"Sweet Jesus is holding you and loving you, Paula."

How she wished she could embrace such belief. Irene was probably the loveliest person she'd ever known. The kids who could run were charging back to the bus. Others came in wheelchairs. Once everyone was aboard Irene clicked on the lights and they played the Christmas songs. What were her little troubles? She sang along with Boney M and *"Mary's Boy Child."* In this moment what did it matter what she believed? There was love and magic in this world. Who couldn't believe in that?

Once the bus was parked and she was back in her tiny flat, the stillness and sense of nothingness crushed her. She stared at her cellphone as she'd been doing twenty-four hours before. She imagined his face. A woman chooses. *A woman chooses.* The phone began to ring but she didn't know the number."

"Paula?"

"Who's this?"

"Vic-the-nick. Listen I just wanted you know something's happened. Poor old Crispin Bissel's in big shit. He went up to Scotland Yard for a career development meeting and got checked at security when he went in. They've found some porn in his briefcase. It's real hard illegal stuff. He's sunk for good."

"That's incredible."

"He's screaming that he's been planted-up but he's got to prove that. Who's going to believe anyone would set him up? Even if he beats the wrap you only have to smear someone these days and they're finished. Any allegation against a bloke is enough."

She was living a horrible fear.

"Vic, I'm hoping this is legit?"

"Of course it's legit. What a mug to just leave that stuff in his briefcase. Anyway the boys just wanted to let you know we care. Jack Miller says you're coming back for the raids. Chin up, gal. Happy Christmas."

She poured a drink. She knew. She knew the boys had stitched him up. She didn't like Crispin Bissel but he was an innocent in a ruthless world. There was no point in worrying. No one would listen to her if she spoke up for him. If any culprit was caught they'd be going to jail and she couldn't support that. They'd be doing DNA, fingerprints and full forensic on the books. She just hoped that no one else would get dragged down by the dogs. The police had changed. Human comradeship had gone and the quest for a higher purity was a filthy business.

Now the room seemed even more oppressive. Perhaps she'd take a walk. A glance out the window revealed a light dusting of snow. She poured another drink. She hated herself for this weakness. When her marriage had failed she'd hit the bottle out of loneliness. She had to drive the community bus in the morning and that would keep a brake on her desire to lose herself. Once the kids were off for the holidays she could let go. She needed to go back to work or make a phone call or both.

A woman chooses.

"Max, Max...."

"I don't care what you were going to say. Stay there; I'm coming over."

"Do you know where I am?"

"Cops are good at questions. Nod three times if you're not at home."

She laughed, bloody hell she was half drunk.

"I'll be there in ten minutes. And thank you."

"For what?"

"For choosing."

She jumped in a cool shower and threw on a skirt and blouse. At least she looked half decent. She saw him pull up in a Jaguar XF. The snow was getting heavier. She grabbed a leather jacket and ran to the car.

"Before you say anything I'm sorry and I love you."

"Why do you say that?"

"Once a man says that to a woman he's said all he needs to say. I'm sorry I drove a bulldozer into that house and I know you won't like my socks. I couldn't find any that matched."

"I was just as interested in the love angle."

"'Cause you don't know what you've got 'til it's gone."

"I've missed you, Max."

"Nah, you can't have missed the real me,'cause I haven't been alive since we broke up."

"Thanks for picking me up. I needed you so much."

"Well, I didn't just come over 'cause you're adorable and beautiful and kind. I'm trying to get the house decorated for Justin and Santa needs an elf to help."

"What's the pay?"

"Mince pies. All you can eat."

Once inside the house he took her into his arms. Nothing else mattered now. Could a woman her age fall for someone so heavily and so quickly? He kissed and stroked as if she were precious. All resistance had fled, waving cheerfully like kids on an outing as they disappeared into the distance.

"Max, I'm simply going to give this all I've got. I've had a couple of vodkas so my brains are a bit loose. Are you straight up going to do the same? We're not kids and I've never been one for trembling on the edge."

His expression was serious.

"Yes. You have my absolute word on that, Paula."

"Then we'd better get on with these decorations. Life might get busy after tomorrow. When does Justin come home?"

"The minute I know for sure that all the McCarthy family is locked up."

"That should be by Christmas Eve."

"There's a fresh bare tree in the lounge. Let's go."

They worked away until midnight. Eventually they stood back to admire the effect. Max wasn't a man to hold back if he wanted something. She'd never seen so many lights and baubles. She had to admit it was fantastic. Through the windows she could still see falling snow. All she wanted to do now was to lie down and snuggle her man and let the universe do its worst.

She lay with her head on his chest. She had an emotion of total trust and protection. There was no urgency to make love and that added to her sense of serenity. The snow deadened all sounds.

"Do you ever wish you could stop time?" he asked.

"Not until now."

"Me too. I've always been dashing on 'cause the unknown prize has always been just ahead. Now I'm holding it."

"I'll always be here to hold, if you want that."

"Will you spend Christmas with us?"

"Try getting rid of me. What do you want as a present?"

"Socks. In pairs."

# CHAPTER 16

She slid the bus through the slush, handed out the chocolate Santas and said goodbye to everyone until the New Year. She got home with a treasure of cards, and gifts of soaps and chocolates. She went through the handwritten messages and drawings. How she would have loved a child. Surely she was too old now and she'd tried with her husband during their marriage. Everything still worked and she'd just gone for it with Max. She could dream couldn't she?

It was mid-afternoon when she got an SMS from Jack Miller.

*"You're on the team. Come in regular civilian dress at midnight. We go in at 4:00 a.m. Get some sleep."*

She called Max. He was going to be at his depot.

"How are you going to get your trucks loaded once you lose all your staff?"

"This close to Christmas everything is already out there. I've got a plan anyway. You stay safe, Paula. I love you."

"I'll catch up with you as soon as I can. I love you too."

There, she'd said it. And she meant it. She tried to sleep, but her mind churned with a problem. All her difficulties had begun when she'd shown Leroy Prentice a shred of mercy. She believed that she'd acted out of natural justice. It was Christmas and Crispin Bissel's life was in ruins because he was too young and inexperienced. He had a chance to learn and grow. She hated him, but she couldn't live with such an injustice in her heart. She picked up her cellphone.

"Complaints and Discipline department?"

"Yes," answered a male voice.

"I'm PC 866L, Paula Middleton. You've got a file on an Inspector Crispin Bissel. He was planted up. I'll die before I tell you who did it but I'll give you a statement to confirm that a person has confided that in me. I know that what I'm telling you is true."

"You could get caught up in the gear wheels of a very nasty machine."

"Do that to me if you want. I don't like the guy and I think he despises me, but there's no second-class species of justice. You treat me as you wish, but I'm telling you all I'm ever going to tell you."

"Paula, I'm chief inspector on this unit. You walked me as a puppy at Brixton eight years ago. I'm getting this file and I'm shredding it because I respect you. Luckily it hasn't been booked in. Now my future is in your hands."

"Guv'nor—will you let him know? The guy's an absolute prick, but I don't want an innocent kid sat with this on his plate for Christmas dinner."

"I'll call him now and tell him there's been a development and that he's off the hook. I'll whisper in an ear upstairs because it may not be good politics to post him back to you."

"Thanks for that. I'm not going to ask your name because I can't sink you if I don't know who you are. Happy Christmas, guv."

And then she slept.


A mob of guys met her as she walked into the station. The sergeant handed her back her police warrant card in an ad hoc ceremony. There was a cheer and calls for a speech. By 1:00 a.m. there was standing room only in the briefing room. Arty types in tight jumpers with BBC press passes and TV gear, swung microphone booms as they crept around making hand signs. Jack Miller opened the show.

"Ladies and you rabble of testosterone-soaked thugs, good morning."

There was a brash roar of laughter. A Scotland Yard media guy flapped frantically at the old detective.

"That's fucking sexist, Jack. There ain't no ladies here," called a voice.

These guys were savages, but she loved them as brothers. Jack Miller got a grip.

"Welcome to our colleagues from the BBC. As citizens we share common goals of justice, truth and similar unbranded products at lower prices. We're delighted and humbled to see familiar household names like Tamara Snidebottom and Jolyon Slyster here tonight. Now, our colleague from media relations is going to do a few words to camera, so can you ignorant barbarians shut your mouths for ten minutes.

The polished media-cops did a pitch on the joy of Christmas and how this spirit had guided the humanitarian policy of the compassionate and gender neutral commissioner. The BBC guys got a sound bite and signalled him to finish. Even they couldn't take too much hype and saccharine-spin. Then different commanders got down to police business. Teams were allocated to hit the places where slave workers would be sleeping. Other teams would be kicking in the doors of the McCarthy clan. A squad was going in to Meadowchef Foods with Basher and Vic-the-nick leading the way. Paula smiled to see that Jack Miller had chosen guys who knew and respected Max.

A female detective inspector from the vice squad gave her briefing.

"Paula, you're with me. When girls come in they'll have to be documented, searched, and interviewed. All females will be going to Paddington Green. We're going to need a lot of paper, pens, and coffee. We're also going to need interpreters and we can expect long delays. We might just get a Christmas lunch in a police canteen if we cook it ourselves."

As the shape of the project unfolded it was evident that it was huge. They could expect up to one hundred and fifty trafficked workers and thirty arrested criminals. Over and above her own future, a big question formed in her mind. When the drama and questioning was over, what were they going to do with all these poor souls? Quite likely it would be Christmas Day. Christmas. Who the fuck needed Christmas?

When the briefing ended, police personnel carriers in the parking area were loaded up with battering rams and big flashlights. Men and woman constables strapped on belts of pepper gas, handcuffs, and batons. The TV cameras licked the dripping juice of the drama and adrenalin. This was going to be one hell of a show and the first footage would hit the screens with the cornflakes. As in all war zones there was a problem. One of the battle-buses didn't have a driver. The media had seized the ticking clock tension. Jolyon Slyster held his watch to camera for those who had no concept of directional time.

*"As the seconds drip, drip away, can a driver be found? Will the vital crew get away to meet their critical deadline?"* he intoned.

Paula eased into the driving seat. She could get to Paddington Green after the action. The cameras lost interest. Guys were checking automatic firearms.

*"Primed for action. These heroes don't see themselves as Santa's little helpers but these fearsome weapons could bring peace and goodwill to our fellow men, women, and those in transition, this inclusive colored Christmas,"* exuded Tamara Snidebottom.

A wispy-bearded crouching producer clasped himself in simpering ecstasy.

Paula fired up the motor. God, it would be great to get out of here and get into a fist fight with criminals.

"This is your captain speaking. Welcome aboard. We'll be flying at a height of about three feet. Does anyone know where the fuck we're going?" she said.

"Streatham Vale. Thanks for stepping in to take the lead. What's your name?" called an officer behind her in the darkness.

"Fucking Rudolph. Who did you expect?"

The team laughed and laughed. She was what she was and what else could she ever be?

"You lot can call me Paula."

She followed shouted directions to a big townhouse. The team went in with the ram and dragged out Ross McCarthy. She'd love to tell Max that she'd helped to scoop the guy who'd torched his Bentley. As luck would have it there were a couple of teenage girls in the house. It seemed they had very little ability in English. She left their prisoner at Brixton and took the two girls and an escort north of the river to Paddington Green police station. Already a crowd of young neglected and often bruised girls was forming in the custody suite. BBC cameras swept their faces.

*"This is the face of modern slavery. Exclusive on this channel the caring services of non-judgemental social management intervene to offer the esprit of seasonal spirituality to these children,"* said Tamara Snidebottom.

At last the TV crews collected their equipment and fled with their sound-bites and video to hit the breakfast shows with a major scoop. Paula had time to grab a coffee and clear a space to work. It was forty hours until Christmas morning. She'd no presents for anyone and she had no idea where she would be. She was a cop. What else?

# CHAPTER 17

One by one the girls were processed. Tales of kids lured to London on false promises of work, then rape, sale to gangsters, and prostitution piled up into a mound of human despair. A couple had been raped and abducted and then smuggled into the country. Some had paid traffickers to get them in, believing they would gain a brilliant life of homes and money. Some girls had just been sold on to work in the beauty business.

At midday she took a break to call Max.

"You must be exhausted," he said.

"I'm getting that way."

"I miss you. I need you."

"That's why I called. Just wanted to make sure you still cared."

She clicked off. Suddenly she had so much in her life and so many had so little. She worked on until mid-afternoon.

"That's it for you, Paula. You've done a top job. There's a de-brief at five o'clock at Brixton and then you're out of here for Christmas," said her inspector.

"That means I've still got a day to do some shopping."

Her mind was a complete blank. She wanted her man and that's all she wanted. She was happy to accept a ride back to her own territory. The first person she saw was Chief Superintendent Jack Miller. He opened his arms to hug her.

"Happy Christmas. Did you hear about Crispin Bissel?"

"Yeah, I can't say we got on but...."

"They dropped it and he's got a new posting to the dog section. With a bit of luck a mutt will bite his ass."

"Goodwill to all men, guv!"

"You OK with Max?"

"I think so."

"I'm pleased for you. He's a rough diamond but in this life there aren't too many diamonds."

She settled down for the meeting. The absence of media made the atmosphere more natural and positive. The immigration guys gave their report.

"Seventy-nine people of which seventeen female recovered and processed. Countries of origin range from Afghanistan to Vietnam via Rwanda. The Home Office of Her Majesty's government have extended temporary permission to remain to everyone. That doesn't mean they won't be deported but they're secure for now. Guys, this is a lot of humanity all in one go but it's just a grain of sand in a universe and we all know that. Merry Christmas."

Jack Miller gave the police perspective.

"All the McCarthys are banged up. We've busted their brothels, cannabis farms, and slave employment agency. With a bit of luck we'll nail them for sexual offences against minors. I just want to acknowledge the input from Paula Middleton who got this enquiry rolling."

There was a cheer from the room.

"The bosses at Scotland Yard were delighted with the stuff that went out on TV and the public have responded with offers of help for the poor sods we've set free. Now it's onwards to the next show. We've got a stabbing and a fatal car accident rolling as we speak. I wish you all a wonderful Christmas."


Now she was truly exhausted. Outside it was dark and more snow was falling. She'd grown so used to being alone that she realized that she still wasn't factoring Max into her life.

"I hope you're waiting for me and not a 45 bus?"

She spun round to see him.

"Max, bloody hell, Max."

"I was in the lobby. You walked right past me."

He held her as snowflakes melted on her skin and turned his dark hair to white.

"Let's go home," he said.

He'd parked the Rolls-Royce a short distance away. As he got in, Justin launched himself from the rear seat to hug her.

Why the hell was she in tears? The lovely smooth vehicle eased its way through the traffic. They could just take her away and she wouldn't raise a finger.

"I picked up Justin on the way to get you. Rachel's gone home for the holidays. He's not seen the house yet. I wanted you to be there."

She smiled at him and inwardly to herself. This young man would never lose the innocent joy of Christmas.

The house was in darkness as they went in. Max threw the switches and the place transformed into a magic of absolute excess. The lad's face lit up even brighter than the lamps. She held out her arms to him as he ran to her.

"Not too much Justin, I saw her first," said Max.

She hardly had the strength to eat. He ran a bath and led her upstairs and sponged her back. Then he put her to bed.

"I've got to deal with Justin. I've not seen him since he went off to Manchester. We'll man-out for a while and I'll get him settled for the night. I love you."

This was a good, good man. Could he really be hers?

And then there was wonderful oblivion.


A powerful hand was stroking her hair and shoulders in her dream. She could smell tea, liquid hot tea. She'd never consciously smelled tea, but she knew what it was. How strange it was in the half-light of a curtained room. Lips were on her cheek.

"I always wanted to find a sleeping beauty."

She started to focus.

"What's the time?"

"Nine."

"Day or night? What shift am I on?"

"Bed shift. It's Christmas Eve and you're all mine for the holidays."

She'd slept for over twelve hours. She could remember the Christmas lights with Justin, and getting in a warm bath. He was seated on the edge of the bed. She stroked his arm. His muscular power gave her a little surge.

"Christmas Eve. I've got to hit the shops."

"I'm going down to the stables with Justin, so you can take your time."

In thirty minutes she was out of the house. She caught the Number 12 service to Regent Street and made her way to Hamleys, the definitive toy store. She hit Oxford Street with no idea of what to get for Max. Well, he was a man who had everything anyway.

By dinnertime she was wrapping presents and by bedtime she was thinking of Christmas dinner. Christmas bloody dinner! What the hell were they going to do?

"Max, I know this is crazy but I've only just thought about turkeys and stuff."

"KFC might be open."

"What?"

"That's what they have in Japan at Christmas."

"Can we get to Tokyo?"

"I kind of run a food business. We might be OK."

His expression was playful. She'd been thinking so much of herself and her work. She'd subconsciously known Max would have fixed things but she was appalled at her lack of awareness of regular life. Until a few days ago she would have expected to cover Christmas shifts for guys who had families and kids, and then grabbed whatever and whenever. To outsiders she must have seemed like a zombie. Suddenly she was a part of a family and that would take some getting used to.

He held her as she relaxed with him in bed. He seemed to love to stroke her as if she were a pet. His hands were tireless and were learning all her pleasure points. He had found more than she had thought possible. She had found more feeling for him than she believed any heart could hold.

"Is this it now? Is this where my life is?" she asked.

"No. There's always a factor X in whatever you plan. I'm not planning to run Meadowchef Foods for always. This would be a good time to sell and I've had offers from a couple of multi-nationals. You may decide to stop being a cop. You could...."

"Don't say that, Max. Don't."

"OK, I won't."

"Thanks."

"But you never know."

"It looks like I'm going to have to shut you up with a kiss."

She rolled onto him and kissed him deeply. Her touch had aroused him and just his presence had primed her. He knew how to find her spot. She watched his face soften as his eyes closed in bliss. A sweeping pleasure in her body blocked any complicated thought. You never did know, did you?

# CHAPTER 18

Justin's joy at his iPhone X was overwhelming. How did the kids get so fast with this stuff? He unwrapped his present from Paula. The first person to respond was Max.

"Wow! It's a remote control shovel excavator. What gave you that idea?"

"Just thought it might develop a useful skill."

The lad hugged her. Max was already getting set up to play with it.

"You could knock a house down with this," he said with a powerful laugh.

"So what about lunch? I smell no turkey cooking."

"I thought we'd go out to the country."

Justin was jumping up and down obviously bursting with some powerful information he'd been ordered not to release.

"I've got you a present," she said.

"We'll be back later and I've got you a little box too. Can we do it later?"

They piled in the Jaguar XF and headed south. The snow has stopped but all the open land and roofs were white.

"Nearly there." Justin was exploding.

They were approaching the stables at Epsom. From some distance she could see a mass of Christmas lamps in a big pine tree that stood at a corner of the yard. They swept in through the gates. All the outbuildings were lit up and decorations sparkled from everywhere that could hang a bauble. He led them through the yard to a brick-built barn set out with a long trestle table with straw bales as seats. She counted places for thirty four people. A few men were setting out place mats, drinking glasses and Christmas crackers.

"Who are these guys?"

"You'll see."

Max led the way into the house. A man was singing a song in some unknown tongue and pulling a turkey out of an Aga oven to baste it. Inside the cavernous interior were several more. Other men were chopping vegetables. An old guy came to shake everyone's hand.

"Happy Krishtlindjet," he said.

"Max, are these the guys from the Meadowchef depot?"

"Sure are. Can't run the place without staff."

"How did they get here?"

"Dad got them all from different places. We went all over," said Justin.

"Well, where do they live?"

"I've patched up some stables we weren't using and put in heaters. I've partitioned the big barn and there's some rooms in the house. I've brought in some prefabricated shower and toilet units so we're all set, at least in the short term. Everyone's been offered a job and they get to keep the wages."

"I'm astounded."

"Money solves everything."

"Money and a big heart."

"Look, Paula, Meadowchef is only one of my companies. I guess I closed my eyes a bit to what was going on and I'm ashamed of that. When young Wayne got his bloody lip, it wasn't because they'd come to see me. After I'd met you I went to see them to tell them they were history. I owe these guys and this is what I can do. It's Christmas with goodwill to all men."

"There's a lot of guys here. Are you worried about trouble?"

"There's a lot of men where you work and it seems OK. A few months ago a guy tried it on at the depot. I dealt with him man-to-man. All these gentlemen know my character. I've appointed a couple of deputies and the men respect them. End of story."

"I love you for this, Max."

"Only for this?"

"Maybe 'cause I'm not having to cook lunch."

The meal was superb. Max sank a few beers, but she offered to drive. She wasn't going to drink for a while. She didn't know the reason but she'd lost the taste and it smelled too strong. Afterwards a couple of guys sang and played guitars. Paula got talking to a bearded young man from Uzbekistan.

"Mr Max, he give everyone envelope. Christmas bonus one hundred."

Before they left, Max shook every hand and looked every man in the eye. There was something in his bonhomie that other men recognized as dominance. She was so glad to be a female around him. They drove home on empty roads, as if the world had stopped. He opened up his computer to watch the Queen's Christmas message.

"Is that part of your traditional code?" she asked.

"Sure is."

Justin divided the rest of the day playing excavators with Max and high-speed navigation of the apps on his new iPhone. The day had been exhausting and she was happy to be alone with him at last.

"I got you a couple of things. I had no idea what you've got."

He unwrapped his parcel. There was a Dolce and Gabbana Bordeaux baroque scarf and a large pack of plain black socks.

"Every sock is a pair. No possible complaints," she explained.

"Paula, you had so much going on and you still thought of us. You're a special woman. Thank you so much."

He appeared to be unsure of how to move forward. He stood up and paced about a little.

"Look, I got you a present and now I'm not sure if it was the right thing to do."

"Getting me a present is always the right thing to do."

He smiled.

"Women are difficult."

"So you got me a book on feminine psychology and you want me to read to you in bed?"

"I didn't, but would you?"

"No, we're finished."

"OK. Here goes."

He went to his office and came back with a flat box. He sat watching her with his hands tightly clasped on his knees. She unwrapped a jewellery box which was something quite large. She peeped inside. It was a Cartier diamond set white gold necklace. She gasped as she pulled it out.

"My God, Max."

Something loose was hanging from it. She turned it to see a fabulous solitaire white gold diamond ring.

"If I want something I just do it. Sometimes I don't always see the other person's point of view. The ring is there in case you ever want to wear it. If not, you can leave it on that chain."

"Max, Max, I'm really struggling with this...."

"I'm sorry. I know I'm too pushy."

"You're perfect. I'm struggling 'cause I'm crying and I can't undo the clasp to get it on my finger."


Fin.

# A MESSAGE FROM EMMA

Hello,

Thank you for reading '*SANTA*' I hope you enjoyed it!

**Please would you help me?**

If you liked the book you've just read, I'd be forever grateful if you'd consider posting a short review. As an independent writer you guys really matter to me. It's very difficult for small authors to get visibility in the huge publishing machine, since we don't have the influence or advertising budgets of traditional publishers. Your review will give me a positive push and help other readers find a book they would enjoy.

Nothing long or complex is needed—just a sentence or two about what you enjoyed about the book.

**Review Link: http://www.smarturl.it/SantaReview**

Why not discover the stories all the other sassy female cops in the Passion Patrol? Check out the next section for links to other books in the Passion Patrol Series as well as a **free book** if you join my mailing list.

Many thanks for your interest in my stories.

*Emma x*

# A FREE BOOK FOR YOU...

## FREE DOWNLOAD

Meet the Passion Patrol Team

**Get this full-length suspense romance novel**

**FREE**

**when you line up with The Passion Patrol**

**...Join Emma Calin's VIP Reader Club**

★★★★★

*"Emma Calin has written another gripping romantic suspense with plenty of both."*
P. Rees-Rohrbacker

Get My Free Book

If you enjoy my books, keep up to date with new releases, special offers and exclusive opportunities. As a valued reader, I'll send you a FREE e-book from my Passion Patrol Series – suspense romance novel GUILT. I email out a few newsletters each month with news snippets and background info to my stories, as well as sharing any bargains. Don't worry I will not bombard you! You may of course unsubscribe at any time.

Link: http://www.smarturl.it/LeadFromSanta **Or scan the QR code:**

# OTHER TITLES BY EMMA CALIN:
# PASSION PATROL SERIES BOX SET 1

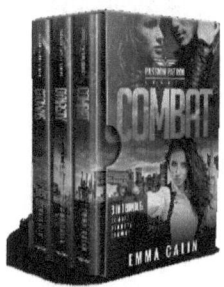

Grab the first three books in the *Passion Patrol Series* PLUS the companion cookbook to the second in the series in one **bargain** bundle. Titles included: *Combat, Dynasty, Seduction of Taste* and *Crowns.*

### http://www.smarturl.it/webbox1

Or if you prefer to buy each ***Passion Patrol*** title individually...

***Guilt, Combat, Crowns, Santa, Wealth, Power***

***Seduction of Taste***

***Seduction of Dynasty Plus*** (2-book bundle, Dynasty+Seduction of Taste)

*Coming in 2019:* ***Desire***

# COMBAT

An early title in the *'Passion Patrol Series'*

Interpol cop, Anna Leyton, spirals down into a hopeless vortex of sexual and emotional passion as she fights to keep her professional cool. Who is deceiving whom in this fast-moving ride across continents? What motivates her art-loving prize bull of a lover, Freddie La Salle? The power of love and trust stands against greed and crime as conflicting forces grapple for that knockout punch.

A romance novel with a twist of suspense that will take you on a roller-coaster ride of passion, deception and love.

**Link: http://www.smarturl.it/webcombat**

**Or scan QR code:**

# DYNASTY

A sexy aristocrat. A wild-child inner city cop. A crime wave of passion.

**http://www.smarturl.it/webdynasty**

**Blurb:**

*A steamy romance novel introducing a sassy female police officer who locks up criminals and always gets her man.*

Moved out from the city after one-too-many maverick missions, Shannon discovers there's more going on in the sleepy country village than meets the eye. The son of a local aristocrat arouses suspicion of drug crime activity... but his widower father arouses more animal instincts!

Could she really mix with the British Royal Family? Can she risk her heart and career on yet another high-risk unauthorized investigation? Can she get justice for an innocent boy? Dare a kid from the gutter dream of being a countess?

Wild child inner city cop Shannon Aguerri walks a dangerous line between her methods and justice. When the bosses lose their nerve, she is transferred to green pastures to play out the role of a routine village cop. In Fleetworth-Green she encounters signs of people and drug trafficking and homes-in on serious millionaire criminals. As a loner she has attracted men but nothing has stuck. When she meets Spencer, the hunky and widowed Earl of Bloxington, there is an immediate rapport between them. Their social differences mean nothing to their passion and need. Already in the mix is an upper-class female rival who has long plotted her way into the earl's bed. The jealousy is an evil shade of green and the anger is a violent scarlet.

Often inhibited by a sense of duty and honor, Spencer is slow to reveal his feelings. When Shannon confronts him with the need to choose between her word and that of her rival, he does not immediately support her. All the same, when they are forced together to carry out a desperate rescue mission, their love is stronger than everything ranged against them.

Please note: This book contains joyful sex between adults in a consenting relationship. There is also strong language in high-stress police confrontations with criminals.

**http://smarturl.it/webdynasty**

# SEDUCTION OF TASTE

Hot Cops. Hot Crime. Hot Romance..... Hot Food?

http://www.smarturl.it/CopsKitchen

SEDUCTION OF TASTE is the companion cookbook to the hot romance novel *DYNASTY*.

A total of thirty-one recipes from appetizers and main courses to suggestions for sandwich fillings at a traditional afternoon tea. Late night suppers and romantic meals for two.

As tough girl cop Shannon Aguerri abandons herself to love with a sexy aristocrat, many meals are shared. From the finest cuisine fit for royals, to the big power passion patrol fuel served in police canteens, SEDUCTION OF TASTE gives you the recipes. You won't want to put the novel down.

With the cookbook you can tickle your taste buds as Emma Calin's full on total romance tickles your mind. If it touches the lovers' lips in the story, you can experience that moment with a meal cooked for your own special lover, be they a cool cucumber or a passionate pepper.

*Read the romance, feel the passion, taste the love!*

Or, grab the bumper gourmet edition—with both the story and recipe books combined and linked together though hyperlinks – *Seduction of Dynasty Plus*.

Jump between the story and the recipes or refer back to the story to re-live those steamy moments whilst you're cooking.

# SANTA

For merciless people traffickers...

... Christmas doesn't exist.

Mature community cop Paula has a heart of gold, a heart broken by love. When gangsters force tough business man Max Muswell to hire exploited labour, Paula steps up to fight at his side.

Love forces up like snowdrops as the Christmas lamps turn on.

Poor and powerless workers face a cold and joyless future. Ruthless crooks fight back as Max and Paula face them down.

*Can an unlikely Santa bring hope and joy?*

Buy this book now to feel spirit of Christmas at any time of year.

**http://www.smarturl.it/websanta**

# GUILT

Gunfire....

...A police dog is down.

Lonely dog handler Helen carries the guilt of survivor. Star singer and single father Marco is too guilty to sing. Both are too guilty to love.

They meet as an innocent animal fights for life. *Perhaps a hope is born?*

Terror fanatics close in on London, their target the Queen. A cop must follow her orders. A father must protect his child.

Love breaks laws and hearts.

Follow the lust and drama. Let go of the guilt. Enjoy the thrill of the action. Follow Marco and Helen to the climax of passion. Hold on for the ride to the triumph of love.

**http://www.smarturl.it/webguilt**

# WEALTH

Masked gunmen strike an exclusive sports car.

Police pursuit interceptor Kaitlyn Thorn takes control.

She snaps the cuffs on the driver, gorgeous cocky Randolph Quinn, the world's richest banker. He doesn't make small talk but he wants to make love.

Sackman-Platinum bank launder the dirty sheets of the underworld. They know where the bodies are buried. As Kaitlyn throws off all sexual chains, she surrenders to pleasure, wealth and intrigue with Randolph.

Police chiefs let her run, encouraging her wild erotic passion for her man and money. In London, Paris, Milan and New York, Kaitlyn exposes herself to a wild trail of evil and greed.

*Is everything what it seems?*

*Could lust, riches and sexual pleasure hide a simple heart in love?*

**http://www.smarturl.it/webwealth**

# POWER

A thug pulls a knife on a mean London street. Police constable Olivia Johnston-Denny faces him down. A regular day. When irresistible American congressman Jackson T Paine intervenes, her life is changed forever. A spark of attraction starts an inferno of erotic heat.

In a world of bitter political division and deceit, this one man offers straightforward country-style honesty. Tipped as a future president, ruthless opponents plot his downfall, by smear or by death. Olivia and Jackson cannot risk involvement but forces of emotion and passion run out of control.

A merciless kidnap and gangster style international bankers fill Olivia's working days. Only in the shadows can she express her love for Jackson.

When her professional investigations lead to her lover's door she stands at a dark abyss. Is he everything he seems?

She has to know the truth as a cop and as a woman in love.

http://www.smarturl.it/webpower

# SUB-PRIME (#1 THE LOVE IN A HOPELESS PLACE COLLECTION)

Two powerless beings are swept together in a transient struggle for survival. Could the human spirit transcend the brutality and indifference of their brief experience before they are once again swept helplessly apart? Far more than a love story—this is a story about love

Sub-Prime: a short story of our times.

Available as an e-book (For Kindle and Kindle Apps for iPad, Android, PC MAC etc.) at Amazon worldwide:

**http://smarturl.it/Sub-Prime**

# THE CHOSEN (#2 THE LOVE IN A HOPELESS PLACE COLLECTION)

A woman, a man, a van, and a plan. When the luck runs out; the lucky walk away. A short story set in the extremis of everyday.

Available as an e-book (For Kindle and Kindle Apps for iPad, Android, PC MAC etc.) at Amazon worldwide on the following link:

**https://www.emmacalin.com/ChosenThe**

# ESCAPE TO LOVE (#3 THE LOVE IN A HOPELESS PLACE COLLECTION)

A woman on the run from domestic violence with no one but her vulnerable autistic teenage child as a companion lives in isolation and fear. While her hand-to-mouth scenarios are played out in the shadow of a threatening suspense, a story of crime and love unfolds around her.

# ANGELA (#4 THE LOVE IN A HOPELESS PLACE COLLECTION)

A mystery tale of a late-night taxi ride where the final passenger may not be all that she seems.

**http://www.smarturl.it/shortAngela**

# LOVE IN A HOPELESS PLACE (#5 THE LOVE IN A HOPELESS PLACE COLLECTION)

A mature woman finds the truth of herself. She cannot go back even though physical and emotional violence erupt around her.

Dare she give in to love?

Will sexual passion and fear overwhelm her stable life?

Whom can she trust to love her for herself?

**http://www.smarturl.it/LIAHP**

# THE LOVE IN A HOPELESS PLACE COLLECTION

Emma Calin's complete set of short stories and novelettes, available in one bargain "boxed set." This edition includes SUB-PRIMe, THE CHOSEN, ESCAPE TO LOVE, LOVE IN A HOPELESS PLACE and short story: ANGELA. It is available as a paperback and e-book from Amazon Worldwide.

http://www.smarturl/it/LIAHPCollection

# CHILDREN'S BOOKS BY EMMA CALIN

### THE "ONCE UPON A NOW!" SERIES

The "ONCE UPON A NOW!" books form a series of illustrated, interactive children's stories, in the true fairy tale tradition with modern-day settings. Each is available in paperback, Kindle, and audio book formats. Digital versions come with clickable links to bonus video clips, photos, and drawings to color. The paperback has QR codes to scan and take you to the same bonus material to enrich the stories.

**http://smarturl.it/OUANAmazon**

Coming soon... The complete Box Set of all three books in the *"Once Upon a Now Series"* for Kindle. Grab this bargain bundle here:

**http://www.smarturl.it/OUANBoxed**

# ALF THE WORKSHOP DOG

How could a scruffy dog in a bus depot, and the call of crows link back to another world of power and love? The ancient Kingdom of Zanubia and a stray dog looking for scraps in an inner-city repair garage, hold the secret. A wicked king, a beautiful girl, a young prince and the struggle between right and wrong maintain the fable tradition.

**http://www.smarturl.it/Alf**

# ISABELLA'S PINK BICYCLE

There's something strange in the woodshed....

A poor little girl in a faraway land dreams of riding a pink bicycle. When she meets a strange animal, her dreams come true. Her happiness turns to sadness when a tragedy occurs in the town and her father doesn't come home. Maybe her new magic friend can find him?

**http://www.smarturl.it/IsabellaPink**

# KOOL KID KRUNCHA AND THE HIGH TRAPEZE

Charlie finds it tough when his parents divorce, but Auntie Kate helps him overcome his greatest fear.

When Charlie has to move from the country into the city, he leaves behind his home, his mates, and his beloved football team. He will need to make new friends. With his small size and red hair, some people aren't kind to him. He wonders if he can face another day at school.

A trip to the circus gives him the strength to see himself and others in a new way.

**http://www.smarturl.it/Kruncha**

# ABOUT EMMA CALIN

Novelist, philosopher, blogger, poet, would be master chef. A woman pedaling between Peckham & Pigalle, in search of passion & enduring romance.

Emma Calin writes romance novels, gritty short stories and children's fiction about love and survival in the 21st century. She has published a number of digital, paperback, and audio books which are available from Amazon and other good bookstores worldwide.

She blogs about her dual life in St-Savinien sur Charente in Southwest France and Romsey, a market town in southern England. She feels extremely lucky to be able to experience the world and life through these two very different lenses. She spends any time she can, when not writing, on her tandem exploring the countryside.

Emma also records and produces audio books and plays the trombone (although not at the same time).

# FIND EMMA CALIN ON THE INTERNET:

Website: **http://www.emmacalin.com**

Blog: **http://emmacalinblog.com/**

Twitter: **http://twitter.com/EmmaCalin**

Facebook: **http://www.facebook.com/emma.calin**

Facebook Fan Page:
**http://www.facebook.com/Knockout.Romance.Novel**

Goodreads:
**http://www.goodreads.com/author/show/4915751.Emma_C alin**

Amazon Author Page: **http://smarturl.it/EmmaAmazonWorldwide**

# PUBLISHER

This book was published by Gallo-Romano Media. For details of other books and authors or if you would like to submit your book for publishing:

Email: **contact@gallo-romano.co.uk**

Web: **http://www.gallo-romano.com**